Savage Storms

Meesha

Lock Down Publications and Ca$h
Presents
Savage Storms
A Novel by *Meesha*

Meesha

Lock Down Publications
Po Box 944
Stockbridge, Ga 30281

Visit our website @
www.lockdownpublications.com

Copyright 2020 by Meesha
Savage Storms

Lock Down Publications
Like our page on Facebook: Lock Down Publications @
www.facebook.com/lockdownpublications.ldp
Cover design and layout by: **Dynasty Cover Me**
Book interior design by: **Shawn Walker**
Edited by: **Kiera Northington**

Stay Connected with Us!

Text **LOCKDOWN** to 22828 to stay up-to-date with new releases, sneak peaks, contests and more...
Thank you.

Submission Guideline.

Submit the first three chapters of your completed manuscript to ldpsubmissions@gmail.com, subject line: Your book's title. The manuscript must be in a .doc file and sent as an attachment. Document should be in Times New Roman, double spaced and in size 12 font. Also, provide your synopsis and full contact information. If sending multiple submissions, they must each be in a separate email.

Have a story but no way to send it electronically? You can still submit to LDP/Ca$h Presents. Send in the first three chapters, written or typed, of your completed manuscript to:

LDP: Submissions Dept
Po Box 944
Stockbridge, Ga 30281

DO NOT send original manuscript. Must be a duplicate.

Provide your synopsis and a cover letter containing your full contact information.

Thanks for considering LDP and Ca$h Presents.

Dedication

I'm dedicating this book to all the Black Kings and Queens who lost their lives by the hands of the police. The very people that made an oath to serve and protect are the ones killing unarmed African Americans as if it's a sport. When will it stop? We as blacks are tired of seeing video after video and the officers running free until we take a stand and start tearing shit up. Then, the government, politicians, and whomever else wants to take action. Keep making noise, we have to make them see things from our perspective because they are pretending to be blind. They know exactly what the hell is going on and it's up to *US* to demand change.

RIParadise

Breonna Taylor George Floyd Eric Garner Michael Brown Tamir Rice Alton Sterling Philando Castile Atatiana Jefferson Aura Rosser Stephon Clark Botham Jean Michelle Cusseaux Freddy Gray Oscar Grant Sandra Bland Korryn Gaines Trayvon Martin LaQuan McDonald John Crawford III Ezell Ford Dante Parker George Mann Tanisha Anderson Akai Gurley Rumain Brisbon Jerame Reid Matthew Ajibade Frank Smart Natasha Mckenna Tony Robinson Anthony Hill Mya Hall Phillip White Eric Harris Walter Scott William Chapman II Alexia Christian Brendon Johnathan Sanders and the list goes on.
#BLACKLIVESMATTER

Meesha

Chapter 1

MaKenzie

"It's time for yo' ass to get back to business. Y'all been diggin' in ya asses long enough!" the voice barked through the phone soon as I answered.

"Heat, you must've forgot who the fuck I am! This ain't one of them hoes you talking to, lower your fuckin' tone when you're talking to me."

"Bitch, I'll—"

"You'll what? Not shit! Whenever you feel like calling me something other than Storm or MaKenzie, you may want to think twice about it. I give you nothing but the utmost respect at all times, I want the same from yo' ass, Heat. As far as me slacking on my job, never that. You know what's been going on with my family."

"Grieving time is over. I need y'all back to work, ASAP! There's a long list of niggas that have money on their heads. Time is money, Storm."

"How you gon' tell me how long I need to grieve? I don't know how long it's going to take me to get over the fact my grandmother is not here anymore. But I'd be damned if I sit here and let you determine when it should. My family comes before any amount of money, remember that shit."

"Yo' ass been running around the Windy City, killin' niggas for free, when you could've had over a million dollars if you would've been available to take the damn jobs. Get ya mind right before I give somebody else the fuckin' jobs, Storm."

"I'm not worried about that weak ass threat. My sisters and I are the best on yo' team. Tell that to one of them rookie niggas. They may take you seriously because I don't. Give me a week and we'll be there," I said, hanging up before he could say another word. Lying back on the hotel bed, my mind drifted back to the night I met Romero "Heat" Ramirez.

One night, my twin sister MaKayla and I decided to go out and have a little fun in the streets of Atlanta. We had just graduated from high school and partying with high schoolers was out of the question. Instead, we decided to hit Club Heat. It didn't take much to get inside without an ID, because the nigga at the door was mad thirsty.

As we walked up to the front of the line, murmurs from some bitches standing in wait could be heard. Ignoring all that bullshit, we approached the bouncer at the door. After letting a few people inside, he turned around and couldn't take his eyes off us. His mouth was hanging open and the drool almost rolled off his lips.

"Damn, y'all fine as fuck! Doublemint twins in the flesh!" he said loudly when he walked into my personal space.

I chose a short black mini dress that had a deep v-cut in the front. My girls were sitting up high, and calves were looking strong in my six-inch stilettos. My makeup was flawless, and my hair was bone straight flowing down my back. MaKayla played it safe with an off-the-shoulder green jumpsuit. She had on a pair of open toed silver sandals with the accessories to match. Her hair was identical to mine and her makeup was on point too.

Giving him any type of play was out of the question. I didn't do well with fat niggas. He stood about five foot seven, if that, and his breath smelled like he ate a bowl of shit before he reported to work. The big razor bumps that graced his face and neck didn't make matters any better.

"Thanks," I said, faking a smile while taking a couple steps back so I could breathe. "Can we go in anytime soon?"

"Soon as you agree to let me take you out," he said, smiling from ear to ear.

"I'm trying to fuckin' party! Would you get out of that bitch face and do your job?"

Some ghetto ass hoe was popping off at the lip and I took that as my cue to go inside before I slit that bitch's throat. I was too cute to be fuckin' a bitch up over bullshit. Easing our way around him, me and Kayla entered the club. "Man, I'm all on that tonight," he said, loud enough for me to hear. I laughed and kept walking because chances were very slim for his fat ass.

Nas' "Ether" was bumping through the speakers and the crowd was feeling it in the new millennium. My brother Scony had me *listening to all the old school rap; I fucked with it. We walked slowly through the crowd toward the bar. The layout was nice, and the place was very spacious. It was packed but it was easy to maneuver through all the people.*

Making it to the bar, I got the attention of the bartender as "She Bad" by Cardi B came on. That was my shit and my ass moved automatically when the beat dropped. I was twerking and rapping the words like the track belonged to me.

Momma needs some meal money
Prada bag and heel money
See my ex he still love me
New nigga gon' kill for me
All my chains got diamonds in it
My account got commas in it
Damn daddy, you fine as hell
I hope yo' wallet got condoms in it

I was all into the song when I felt a pair of hands wrap around my waist. Glancing over my shoulder, I made eye contact with the finest nigga I'd ever seen. He stood six feet even, had a caramel skin tone, low tapered haircut, with a goatee that was shaped up razor sharp. His luscious pink lips had me thinking how they would feel wrapped around my clit without even knowing his name. The smell of his Acqua Di Gio cologne filled my nostrils and almost made me cum in my thong.

"Dat ass, dat ass, dat ass, dat ass, she bad, she bad, she bad, she bad," he rapped in my ear as he grinded on my ass.

Usually I would've snapped on a muthafucka that invaded my privacy like that, but I needed to get to know this one. While twerking on his manhood, I felt what he was working with down below. His pipe was sitting on top of his thigh, my type of man.

The song ended and so did our dance. I stood up straight, adjusting my dress in the process. It was a good thing I decided to wear a pair of black Spanx, or my ass would've been out for everybody to see. Kayla was shaking her head as she held out the drink she took the liberty of ordering for me. I took a sip of the Long Island iced tea and winced at how strong it was.

"What's your name, beautiful?" Mr. Handsome asked in a deep baritone as he leaned against the bar. Turning to face him, I caught him licking his lips and my lady parts thumped like a set of drums being beaten.

"MaKenzie, and you are?" I asked loud enough for him to hear me over the music.

"I'm Heat, baby."

I gave him the side eye because I hated when niggas gave me their street names. "Yo' mama didn't give you the name Heat when you were born, try again."

He let out a slight chuckle, showing off his perfect smile in the process. "I usually don't give nobody my gov'ment, but you're too beautiful for me to let you get away. My name is Romero, mamí."

"Nice to meet you, Romero," I said, before we were rudely interrupted.

A thick female stalked over and forced her way between the two of us. She kept looking between Romero and I with a scowl on her face. Waiting for her to speak her peace didn't last long, because disrespect was something I didn't tolerate.

"Excuse you. Is there something I can help you with?" I asked annoyingly.

"Yeah, you can start by telling me why you over here all in my man's face!" she snapped.

The shit was comical because this bitch was big mad. She had shit all wrong, her man was in my face, not the other way around. I laughed and ordered another drink. When I paid the bartender, I got up and looked Romero in the face and said, "Handle that," before I walked away, leaving both of them standing right there.

"I'm glad you didn't entertain that shit, sis. We came here to have a good time, not beat a bitch head in," Kayla said, sipping her drink.

"Sis, you already know I'm too muthafuckin' cute right now. Her ass better be lucky Granny taught me how to laugh stupid shit off and walk away. She may not be too lucky if she tries that shit a second time, though."

We found a seat in an empty booth in the back of the club and sat down. I grooved to the music as I nursed my drink and paid attention to what was going on around me. My eyes landed on Romero and the female at the bar. It looked as if she was going off on him and he didn't seem fazed by whatever she was saying. Romero got in her face and said something to her and walked away.

I could tell she was pissed because her facial expression said it all. Watching him walk away, she gave a signal to someone across the room. I glanced in the direction she was looking but I couldn't pinpoint who she was silently communicating with at first. Romero walked down a hall and three niggas followed him after a while and the female went out the door.

I turned to Kayla and whispered, "Something's about to go down. I think that chick just set Romero up."

"Who the fuck is Romero?" she asked, confused.

"The dude I was talking to at the bar."

As I fumbled around in my purse under the table, Kayla already knew what I was on. "Kenzie, nope. We didn't come here for this shit. You don't even know this nigga! Let's get up and leave this muthafucka!" Ignoring her, I screwed the silencer on my bitch and stood up. "MaKenzie!"

I heard when she called my name and stopped without looking back at her. Kayla wasn't going to let me do this shit alone, we always had each other's backs. A minute or so later, I heard her getting up and I led the way down the very hall that Romero entered. We neared a door with a nameplate mounted to it. The name read "Heat" and it dawned on me that he was the owner of the club.

"Nigga, open the mufuckin' safe!" a voice bellowed from the other side of the door.

"I'm not opening shit! You muthafuckas gon' have to kill me before I willingly give y'all some shit I worked my ass off to obtain!" Heat said without fear.

Looking through the crack in the door, I saw Heat down on his knees in front of an opened closet-like door. I noticed the floor was carpeted when I glanced down at the floor. Slowly removing my Nina, I turned to Kayla, she was already locked and loaded.

13

"Heat, I don't want to kill you, even though I should because of the way you be fuckin' ova my sista. You are lucky my nephew loves yo' half-breed ass. It's the only reason I'm considering letting yo' punk ass live. Now, open the safe!"

"When he opens that bitch, send his ass to hell, Rock! His ass is not gon' sit back and let this shit slide. You outta yo' rabbit ass mind!" one of the other dudes growled.

"Shut the fuck up, I know what I'm doing," Rock screamed.

I whispered to Kayla, "We got to hit these niggas fast. We can't give them time to react. I'm going for the one with the gun to Romero's head, I want you to hit the one standing to his right. The other one that's to the left of my target don't have a gun in his hand, so we have to make sure he never gets the opportunity to draw that bitch."

Kayla nodded her head and I swiftly entered the office sending a bullet into the back of Rock's head. His body fell upon the desk face first with a loud thud.

"What the fuck!" the other guy yelled as he raised his gun. He let off a wild shot as Kayla put two slugs into his chest.

The third guy fell to his knees with his hands in the air. I knew damned well he didn't think surrendering was going to get him out of the bullshit he'd gotten himself into. "Heat, let me explain—"

"Nigga, I'm not trying to hear shit you have to say!" Heat yelled, standing to his feet. "You mufuckas didn't think this shit through, but you'll have plenty of time to think about it now."

POW! POW! POW!

Heat shot him three times in the face and his body slid down the wall slowly as his head slumped to the side. I closed and locked the door as Heat snatched his phone off his hip. His eyes met mine as he waited for whomever to answer.

"Clean up in the office. I dropped three cases of Henny in this bitch," he said, ending the call. "What the fuck were you thinking, coming in here?" he asked angrily.

"Look, shit didn't look good when ya lil girlfriend gave them niggas the go-ahead and bounced. Yo' ass lucky I followed my first mind, or you would be the one lying lifeless in this muthafucka. A

thank you would've been nice though," I said, rolling my eyes as I dismantled my gun, dropping it in my purse.
"Where the hell y'all learn to handle them thangs like that? I could use a couple of sexy ladies on my team who can hold their own better than some of these niggas on the street. It's just what the doctor ordered," Heat said, rubbing his hands together.
"Yo' team?" Kayla asked with attitude.
"Yeah, I want y'all to meet me at this address tomorrow at three," he said, writing on a card he pulled from his breast pocket. "I'll explain everything when you show up. If y'all down to make a couple hunnid grand a job, you'll be there. Until then, shake out of this muthafucka and get at me. My number on the back, beautiful. Give me a call when you get home," he said, handing the card to Kayla.
"Wrong twin, potna," she smirked holding the card out to me. We laughed and headed for the door.
"Thanks for having my back. I appreciate that shit," he said as we made our exit.

That was the night we began killing muthafuckas for a profit. I hadn't come down from that high yet. I had one more mission to complete before we got back to the paper chase. It was time for me to put an end to this nigga Dray's life. I've played around in Massachusetts too damn long.

***

It was my last night to play this game with the punk ass nigga that fucked over my family. Drayton Montgomery had played with Kaymee's life and took advantage of her because she was young and naïve. He should've thought long and hard about who the hell she had on her team. His downfall was for sure pussy.

The night before, I put mine on him to the point his mind was blown. He was able to dick whip Kaymee because he hadn't had that good shit from a real woman. We agreed to meet at my hotel, and I checked out on his ass just to give me the opportunity to break in his house while he was gone. The low budget alarm system he had installed was a piece of cake to bypass.

I sat waiting for him to return home, with nothing but patience. When he walked through the door, I sat comfortably in the armchair without any worry. He was shocked to see me but that turned into pure anger in seconds.

"Hello, Dray. Did you miss me?"

"How did you get in my house?"

"Never answer a question with a question, love," I smirked.

"I'm not trying to hear that shit, MaKenzie. What the fuck are you doing in my house?"

Dray was fuming because his baritone didn't move me. That shit worked with them young bitches, not me. I was a killa and he truly didn't know who he was buffing up at.

"Don't make me repeat myself."

"And if you do, what will happen, Dray? Not nothing. Why I'm in your house isn't important," I said, placing my hands in the pocket of my hoodie. "Why did you lie to me about what you do for a living? I did my homework and you're not a graduate of More-house—"

"I didn't lie to you! What the fuck you doing checking up on me? I've been nothing but good to you."

He pushed off the door like he was going to do something to me. I had to stop him in his tracks before he got too excited and made me kill him before I wanted to. Laughing on the inside, I wanted to push his buttons a bit further to see how angry he would actually get.

"Nigga, if you ever raise your voice at me again, shit will get real funky in this bitch! I need to know who I fuck with at all times, especially when things seem too good to be true. See, for a nigga that just bought a home with no job—"

"I have a muthafuckin' job! I work for Boeing!" he yelled, walking toward me with his fist clenched.

Chuckling loudly, I crossed my right leg over the left as I strummed my tool. "Pipe down, homie. There's no need to get upset because you were caught in a lie. Oh, you can rest your hands, my

16

name ain't Kaymee. You won't get away with putting your hands on me."

Dray stared at me with a hint of fear in his eyes. Sizing me up, I guess he figured because of my size, he would be able to take me. He moved forward slowly, and I stood up and pulled my bitch from my pocket and held it by my side.

"See, Dray, I knew exactly who you were when I saw you at the airport. Not only did you put your hands on the wrong woman, you stole from the wrong nigga in Atlanta. Did you really think you would get away with that shit?" I shot at him with my head tilted to the side.

"That's grown men business. It has nothing to do with you, MaKenzie. If that's your real name," he snarled.

"It has everything to do with me, nigga! For the record, I'm a straightforward bitch. I don't have to lie to make my life seem greater than it actually is. My name *is* MaKenzie, but you can call me Storm," I smiled.

"When you fuck with the Goon Squad, you fuck with me. You were part of the squad for a short period of time and didn't get to meet all the players of the game. There are female goons in that muthafucka, too.

"It wasn't too hard to get close to yo' ass, so that told me you weren't fit to be one of us to begin with. Kaymee is family and you violated in the worse way. You should've been taught not to put yo' hands on a female early in life. Don't worry, you will definitely learn your lesson tonight. Now, where's my muthafuckin' money, Dray?"

"I don't owe you shit, bitch!" he screamed.

Pew! Pew!

"Aaaaahhh, shit!" he yelled out in pain as two bullets entered his left kneecap, dropping him to the floor.

"Disrespect is something I don't do well with, Dray. This should be a valuable lesson to not think about pussy after you've wronged somebody. It throws off your game, but I'm glad you enjoyed the ride I took you on." Standing over him with my pistol pointed downward at his head, I laughed out loud at the tears that cascaded down his face.

"I'll give you the money and the pills! Just don't shoot me again, please. Everything's in the safe in the closet. The combination is zero-seven-one-one. Take whatever is there and leave."

This muthafucka was crying real tears and it was comical as fuck to me. I shattered his knee to the point he would need several surgeries to repair it. Good thing the hospital bill wasn't going to fall on him to pay. I hoped his insurance was paid because he was going to have a hell of a funeral.

"You are a pussy," I laughed in his face. "There was no way you were cut out to be a Goon. If you were robbed back in Atlanta, Kaymee would've died fuckin' with you because the way you're acting now, you would've thrown her to the wolves. I can't stand a weak muthafucka. I'm gonna have fun getting rid of your punk ass," I said, standing up straight.

Grabbing him by the front of his shirt, I dragged him across the floor and he gripped my ankle, causing me to stumble slightly. Lifting my foot, I brought it down on his head and he howled like a wounded dog. Dray released me quickly and I placed the tip of the silencer on the top of his head.

"Get the fuck up!"

"I can't! You shot me!"

"You have to the count of five to get yo' punk ass up. If I make it to five and you're still on the floor, I'm going to put a bullet in your fuckin' head! One. Two. Three. Four. Five."

When I got to five, Dray was standing, leaning on his good leg against the arm of his sofa. He had sweat pouring down his forehead and he was breathing like he ran a marathon. I kind of felt sorry for his ass because he didn't look so tough with hot lead in his leg. In fact, he looked pitiful as hell.

"Get yo' ass in there and get my shit," I said, pointing behind me. He opened his mouth and I cut him off. "Don't say shit else to me, Dray. Move!"

Hopping on his one good leg, the struggle was real for him, trying to get to the closet. He opened the door and used it as leverage while he punched in the code to the safe. Soon as the safe unlocked, I emptied the clip into the back of his head. If he thought I was about to spare his life, he thought wrong.

Collecting everything inside the safe, I wiped down everything I touched and left Dray lying in a pool of blood, where he would be until the Boston police found his ass stankin'.

Meesha

Chapter 2

MaKayla

"Conte, stop! I just finished eating and the food is still sitting on my damn stomach."

Trying to fight my man off me was a task in itself. To be honest, I was tired and really didn't feel like have a long ass sex session. When it came to quickies, Conte didn't know anything about it and because of that, he wasn't getting started if I had anything to do with it. His best bet was to crawl over and go to sleep.

"MaKayla, you trippin'. That's my pussy, and I need it now!"

I couldn't do anything but laugh because he was stupid. Conte and I had been going strong since we met a few years ago. Life was good since our family had gotten rid of all the bullshit that made its way into our lives.

After losing our grandmother, our family's world was like a movie on a weekly basis. First, it was G and Nova's drama, then we had to deal with my brother Scony almost losing his life by our aunt's hands. There was a sense of peace for about a year and we were able to enjoy family, until G found his little cousin Kaymee after not seeing her in years.

The drama started all over again and the family had to come together once again to act as superheroes. Conte had it in his mind that I was in Chicago to stay. He was right about that, but I had a feeling I would have to move around and get back to business very soon. When the time came for me to go back to work, it was going to be a problem on his part.

"Baby, if I give you what you want, will you allow me to get some sleep?" I asked, propping my elbow on the pillow.

"When I lay this pipe on yo' ass, that's exactly what you gon' do," he said, moving between my legs as he kissed me deeply. "You gon' stop depriving me of what is rightfully mine, Kayla. Let me remind you why you've been home all this time."

Easing down my body, Conte pried my legs open and dove face first into my love box. He pushed my legs back toward my head, grasped my clit between his lips and sucked softly. I thrusted my hips forward and palmed the back of his head. The pressure was intense, and I was on the brink of exploding.

"Aaaah, shit! Yessss, baby!" Conte came up just as I was about to downpour on his lips. "You better get your ass back down there! Aht-aht, nigga!" I said, lowering my legs.

"Shut up! Don't tell me how to treat my shit. I'm doing this my way."

Conte growled, pushing my legs further behind my head. He had me folded up like a pretzel and my ass was stuck. I felt the tip of his mushroom head make its way into my opening and I waited for what was about to take place. My man stroked the kitty, with long and slow strokes that took my breath away.

"Fuck! Mmmm," I moaned, holding onto my feet.

"Yeah, I don't hear you talking that shit now. You 'bout to learn today."

Conte fucked me just the way I liked and there was not one lie that spewed from his dick. He got me right for over an hour and a bitch was spent. Usually, I would get up to take a shower, but my body was relaxed and I couldn't do anything but close my eyes and drift off to sleep.

I don't know how long I had been asleep, but my phone ringing jarred me awake. Conte was snoring with his body wrapped around mine and it was hard for me to move my arm to retrieve my phone. I pried his arm from around my waist and wiggled out of his grasp.

"Hello," I answered the phone without looking to see who was calling.

"Wake your ass up so you won't be able to say you didn't talk to me."

MaKenzie's voice boomed in my ear and that prompted me to glance at the time. She was wide awake at one in the morning and I knew it was time to head out for work. Sitting up on the edge of the bed, I looked over my shoulder at Conte before raising up to leave the room.

"I'm woke, Kenzie. Why are you calling me so late?" I asked, sitting on the couch.

"Kay, if I'm calling it's for a reason. I received a call from Heat, and we've been summoned to Atlanta. The tickets are purchased, and we leave at noon. I've tried to contact Nicassy to no prevail. Have you talked to her since I've been gone?"

I sat staring at the wall because I brought the thought of going back out into the streets to work a reality. Conte was going to blow a gasket when I told him. He was under the impression I was going to leave that part of my life alone, but I never agreed. Any time the subject was brought up, I would brush it off by changing the subject.

"Kay, you still there?" my sister asked with an attitude.

"Yeah. Yeah, I'm still here. What happened to giving me a heads up? Things have changed since we did our last job."

"What has changed, Kay? Conte? I know damn well you not about to let him stop you from getting this money. He knew what the fuck you did for a living before y'all got serious. It's not your fault he didn't believe the shit because yo' ass decided to become domesticated while we took a break."

"I'm not worried about him stopping me from doing what I've always done. Don't go there, sis. You should've told Heat to give us a little time so I can talk to Conte. Being domesticated doesn't have anything to do with the disagreement that's bound to occur. It's called communication and priorities. We are in a relationship, something you know nothing about."

"And that's the reason I'm by my damn self. There's no way a nigga would be able to dictate what I can and cannot do with my life. Falling in love is something that's not in my future plans." I could picture my twin rolling her eyes as she talked all that rah-rah shit on the other end of the phone. "You never answered my question, have you talked to Nicassy?"

Thinking back to the last time I talked to my sister by another mister, I couldn't recall the last time. She didn't attend the housewarming in Atlanta for Monty and Poetry and every time I called, she was always busy. I didn't think anything of it until Kenzie mentioned her.

"Actually, I haven't talked to her. It's not like her to go ghost for this amount of time. She's okay, because I've called but she's always busy."

"When I couldn't get in touch with her, I didn't purchase her ticket. She will have to get to Atlanta on her own. I'm about my money. Nicassy is moving like she done got boo'd up like yo' ass. Both of y'all can have that shit. I'm good. Make sure you're ready at nine in the morning, because I'll be there to pick you up on time."

"I can't let you roll alone. Hopefully, there won't be a big drawn out fight with Conte."

"Fighting with me about what. Kayla?" Conte asked calmly from the entryway of the living room.

"Sis, I'll see you in the morning. Get some sleep and you can fill me in on what happened in Boston on the ride."

Ending the conversation with my sister, I sat looking at my phone for a minute before I stood up from the couch. I was dreading having to tell Conte I was leaving for the airport in a matter of hours. He stood with his arms crossed over his chest with a grim look on his face.

"Kayla, what's going on?"

"Let's go in the bedroom. I need to talk to you," I said, squeezing past him and led the way down the hall.

Sitting on the bed, I waited for Conte to join me in our intimate space. The wheels were turning in my head trying to figure out how I was about to keep the conversation on a civil level. Conte and I had no problems but the mention of what I do for a living always hit a nerve.

"What do you have to talk about, Kayla?"

"As you heard, I was talking to my sister when you walked in. Conte, we have to go to Atlanta and I'm leaving in the morning."

Conte was quiet but his body language said a thousand words. The heat was resonating around the room and I knew he was pissed, without hearing me out. Shaking his head, Conte ran his hand down his face and turned to me.

"Going to Atlanta for what? I know you're not going to do what you *used* to do, MaKayla."

24

"Used to do? That's how I make my money, Conte. I'm not about to argue about this with you. I told you all about my job when we first got together."

"You don't have to do that shit no mo'! Kayla, you're my woman and I wouldn't be a real nigga if I sat back, letting you think this is okay. I work hard every day, so you don't have to put your life in jeopardy in the streets. But here you are, trying to go out there doing nigga shit!"

"*You* work hard for yourself! I'm not with you for your money, Conte. Not to throw anything in your face, I've had my own money from the start. Listen, I appreciate you trying to get me out the streets, but the same way you go out and handle your business to make money, so do I."

"What you not gon' do is sit here and try to compare apples to oranges, we are not the same. I'm a man and you're a woman. My woman at that! I'm supposed to be in the streets, you not! Every time I tried to talk about *your job*, you changed the subject and never wanted to discuss it."

"I never discussed it because you knew what the fuck you were getting into when you found out what I did for a living. It was okay when I was doing the shit alongside the Goon Squad. What's the difference now? This didn't just come out of the blue, Conte. I've been killin' muthafuckas for a living since the age of eighteen. I'm almost twenty-two, holding shit down on my own. I don't even allow my brother to dictate what I do with my life, so—"

"I'm not your brother!" Conte took a breath while staring at me. "Look, I don't want you to go back into this type of work. If you want to make money, I'll start whatever business you want. Just say the word and you got it."

"If I wanted to do that, it could've been done a long time ago on my own dime. I love what I do, Conte. The reason I've been sitting back so long is because my family was going through things and I wanted to be there to help. Now, it's time for me to go back to Atlanta to make this money. Plus, I can't let my sister go out there by herself. We've been doing this shit together from the beginning."

Standing to my feet, I went into the closet and retrieved my luggage and placed it on the bed. Nothing was going to stop me from getting on that plane. I went back into the closet and took several outfits from the hangers and folded them neatly before placing them inside the luggage.

"Basically, you're saying fuck me, huh?" Conte asked calmly.

"No, I'm not saying that at all." Without stopping what I was doing, I replied back to him. One part of me wanted to call Kenzie back and say I was done, but the other part of me missed the thrill of taking a life.

"Kayla, if you leave, we are done. I won't live my life worrying myself to death, wondering if you're dead or alive. I'm not gon' do it."

"I can say the same about you, but being a female in this game, I know what the consequences are. Do I worry about you when you're out handling business? Yeah, I do. But I be on high alert and ready to strap up, in case I have to come stand by your side. That's the type of ride or die bitch I am. But you fucked up, trying to throw an ultimatum in my face. You want to walk, handle yo' business, baby."

The words he threw at me finalized my decision. I finished packing for my trip and walked past his ass to put my luggage by the front door. When I returned, he was still standing in the same spot, huffing and puffing. Walking toward the bathroom, I stopped and turned around to see if he had anything else to say. When he didn't open his mouth, I proceeded on my way and closed the door.

Chapter 3

Heat

Opening my eyes, I realized I wasn't in the comfort of my own home. Immediately swinging my legs out of the bed, I sat for a moment until my eyes adjusted to the dark. My mind went back to earlier that night as I tried to figure out who's fuckin' bed I was in. I didn't have to wonder too long because a soft hand to my back let me know I wasn't alone.

"You sneaking out on me?" the female asked groggily.

"Sneaking? Hell nawl, I'm about to leave soon as I find out who the fuck you are," I shot back, fumbling for the switch on the lamp which sat on the nightstand beside the bed.

The light lit up the room and I turned around to the ugliest female I'd ever seen in my life. The mama orangutan's hair was standing straight up on her head, the teeth in her mouth had an overbite that caused me to grab my dick to see if it was still where it supposed to be. I thanked the man upstairs, because at least I had the good sense to double strap with the beast.

"Why you have to say it like that? You act like you wasn't just fucking me into submission a few hours ago," she said, sitting up as the sheet fell down, exposing her titties that damn near touched her flabby stomach.

I almost threw up in my mouth because I had to be fucked up to even be alone in this person's house. Glancing down at the floor, I spotted my clothes in a heap on the floor and made a dash for them without responding to her. I was fully dressed in less than three minutes and that was a record. Shid, I didn't even bother to take the condoms off. Getting the hell out of there was my top priority.

"Samuel, do you hear me talking to you?"

I stared at her like I was hard of hearing because I knew my name wasn't Samuel. Hell, that was a lame nigga's name. I checked my pockets and wasn't shit in them except my phone. Hopefully, my wallet was in my fuckin' car or I'd be back to stomp a mud hole in this bitch for stealing from me.

"Look, I don't know you and I'm about to bounce. I hope you had a great time, because I don't remember shit that happened in this muthafucka. Wherever we met, stay yo' ass away because if I see you again, you gon' come up missing."

Rushing out of her bedroom, I followed my gut to get out of her cluttered home. When I got outside, I slammed the door behind me and took a deep breath as I rushed to my whip. Hitting the key fob to unlock the doors, ole girl stepped out and started screaming at me. I left her ass standing right there to talk that bullshit to herself.

The clock on the dash read six o'clock in the morning and I couldn't wait to get home so I could take a long hot shower. Those long ass titties flashed before my eyes and the urge to vomit was evident in my throat. Saliva kept building up in my mouth and once I was a distance from her house, I pulled over and released everything on my stomach, out on the side of the road.

"You gotta stop this shit, Heat. You allowed the wrong one to pick yo' ass last night," I said, reaching into my armrest for a napkin.

Shaking the image from my thoughts, I traveled the streets of Atlanta fast as I could without drawing attention from the cops, so I could get home. Getting myself together for the meeting I had set up was imperative. Storm and Kane had been stagnant for far too long. I had to put some fire under their ass because it was time to get back to business.

I had too much work that had to be taken care of and my team wasn't as strong as it used to be. I'd lost so many men since the ladies been away. The males are supposed to be the dominate ones, but I hadn't seen shit as of late. The last group of niggas were proving to be just what I needed, and I couldn't wait to see how the team would work together. It was that damn Storm who was going to cause problems. She never wanted outside help but this time around, the choice wasn't hers.

The commute home took thirty minutes. I couldn't believe I traveled so far to smash a big ugly bitch. Pulling up to the gate, I entered the code and drove through when it opened. When I spotted Summer's car, I sighed hard because arguing was one thing I didn't feel like doing early in the morning. Explaining my whereabouts was another. Summer managed Club Heat and she also managed to please me when I needed her to. I regretted giving her access to my shit, but on the other hand, she wouldn't have been there if she wasn't instructed to come. Another thought crossed my mind as to how I ended up somewhere else if I told Summer to meet me at my crib. An explanation didn't come to me and that shit was frustrating. As I entered the front door, it felt like I was creeping in my own place on some sneak type shit. Clicking the lock in place, the smell of coffee was evident in the air and that was my cue Summer was wide awake. I climbed the stairs and pushed the door open to my bedroom slowly.

Summer was sitting up with a mug on her face and I laughed on the inside because she really wanted to be the woman in my life. Unfortunately, she wasn't. Moving around the room silently, I started taking my clothes off so I could take a much-needed shower.

"So, you just gon' come in here like you didn't invite me over and stood me up?"

"I don't feel like going through this with you, Summer. This is my house. I can come in any way I want because I bought this muthafucka, so I can do just that. If I told you to come here, that meant I had intentions to join you, obviously something else came up," I said, pulling my shirt over my head and tossing it in the hamper. I pulled my pants and boxers down and all hell broke loose.

"You a dirty nigga, Heat!" Summer yelled as she jumped out of the bed. "You got me fucked up for real. How about taking the condom off after you finished with the bitch!"

Glancing down at my dick, I'd forgotten how fast I ran out of the mystery bitch's house. Therefore, I didn't think about the jimmy hat I still had hanging from my manhood. I wasn't fazed about it though, all I could do was hunch my shoulders, step out of my pants and walked in the adjourning bathroom.

I turned the nozzle to the shower on and waited for the water to get to the temperature I loved. Grabbing my toothbrush, I put some toothpaste on the electronic gadget and raised my arm when

Summer appeared in the doorway. The bullshit was about to continue, and I had to keep shit leveled because I didn't want to lose her as the manager of my business. Mixing business with pleasure was never a good thing when there was nothing becoming of it.

"Heat, what the fuck are we doing?" she asked.

"What do you mean?" I replied, placing the toothbrush in my mouth.

"We've been doing this for almost two years, and we aren't moving any closer to a commitment. Why are you wasting my time?"

Spitting into the sink, I stared at her through the mirror before responding. "Summer, you are the one that's looking for a commitment. It was never part of my plan. I've told you on so many occasions, not to get in your feelings about what we're doing. How many times have I told you I'm not looking for anything serious?" I asked.

"That's what your mouth says, Heat. Your actions speak something different. Your vibes come off like you're claiming me. Whenever you see anyone in my face, you act as if you want to murder them. If I don't answer your calls, you always accuse me of being with somebody else. Now, you want me to believe I'm just a random bitch. Stop sending mixed signals, nigga! If this shit ain't going nowhere, leave me the fuck alone and stop wasting my time!"

I continued brushing my teeth because when we had this conversation before, she said she understood where I was coming from after we talked. She swore she was cool with my mindset, but that definitely wasn't the case. Rinsing my mouth, I wiped the excess water off with my face towel and turned to face the woman I didn't want to hate me for any reason at all. If anything, our friendship was more important than anything at the moment.

"Look, Summer. I've been nothing but truthful to you. Putting everything on the table from the beginning should've given you an idea how things would play out. A relationship isn't something I want right now. I have things that needs my undivided attention and giving a woman the time, affection, and love she deserves is something I can't provide. It doesn't mean I don't care about you, it's just something I don't want to get myself into, knowing I won't be able to give one hundred percent."

"That shit sounds good, I hear you. I'll leave you to do things your way. Just don't include me anymore."

"This is the reason I wanted to end things the last time we had this conversation. I never want to hurt you, Summer. I cherish our friendship and I don't want this to destroy what we have as far as business is concerned. I'm sorry for putting you through all of this. I think we should remain friends, that's something I can promise we will always have. All that other shit, I won't even pretend to do."

"I hear you loud and clear. I'm going to get out of your hair and take care, Heat."

Summer turned and walked away. I wanted to go after her, but that would give her the impression we could continue on the same path, and I didn't want to give her false hope. Allowing her to leave was the best option, for me anyway.

I shaved until I heard the front door slam and made a mental note to myself to change the code on my front door. The last thing I needed was Summer coming to my home on some other shit because I knew I'd hurt her with my honesty. A woman scorned was something I didn't want to deal with and hopefully, it didn't turn into that.

My intentions were never to hurt Summer, but I understood where she was coming from. Women had feelings that men didn't possess. It was easy for a woman to catch feelings because they were looking for love. But a man could ride the wave and walk away just as easy. It may sound fucked up, but it's the truth.

Stepping into the shower, I let the water run over my entire body before I lathered up and washed completely two times. My muscles relaxed and I was ready to sleep. I looked at the clock on the wall and it was almost eight in the morning. Strolling into my bedroom in all my glory, I climbed in bed. Summer's scent filled my nostrils, but I didn't feel like getting up to change the sheets. I won't lie, it had me thinking about everything with Summer and how I needed to handle the situation.

***

The ringing of my phone me woke up and I rolled over, searching high and low for it. I had to get up and cross the room to retrieve it from the dresser. It was one in the afternoon and I had a couple hours before I had to head to the club for my meeting.

"What up?"

"I thought I'd give you a call to make sure you were good. You left the spot with an ugly muthafucka last night."

"Phantom, how the fuck you let me leave with that thing?" I screamed into the phone.

"Nigga, I tried to tell yo' ass to slow the fuck down. You were adamant about leaving, so I let yo' ass go. Baby girl was all over you," he laughed. "She even polished yo' knob for everyone to see. That mouthpiece had yo' ass gone. I think that's what got you out the door."

Walking back to the bed, I got back in it. "I fucked around and fell asleep at her crib. When I saw her ass, I jumped up and got the fuck outta there. I'm fuckin' you up for not tryin' harder to save me. You in violation because I would've never sent you off like that."

"Heat, you a grown ass man! That big bytch worked yo' ass over and now you're mad at me." Phantom was laughing too hard for me and it was starting to piss me off.

"Be at the meeting on time. I have some shit to discuss, and whatever happened last night won't be one of the subjects. Keep that shit to ya'self. Understood?"

"Yeah, I got it. Don't get fucked up like that again and you won't have those type of problems. I hope you strapped the fuck up, wouldn't want you to be the daddy of a lil monkey baby. That muthafucka would look just like its mama."

"Fuck you, nigga!" I said, bangin' on his ass.

My stomach growled, reminding me that I hadn't eaten anything since the night before. I slapped on a pair of basketball shorts and headed for the kitchen with my phone in hand. When I got to the bottom, I remembered Summer leaving in a huff, and went directly to the app in my phone to change the code on my doors.

Bacon, eggs, and toast was calling my taste buds and I was ready to make that shit come to light. Taking out the ingredients I would need from the refrigerator, I started doing what I had to do to eat. I finished cooking my breakfast and sat down checking my email as I ate. There were quite a few jobs that came through and business was booming.

I was kind of glad MaKenzie and MaKayla was coming back because some of the niggas weren't cutting it in my shit. I'd never seen so many men that couldn't pull a trigger successfully. It was a disgrace to me and what I'd built. I've also made a new enemy in the streets that I had to bring to the team's attention. No one knew the players in my circle, but it was imperative I filled them in on what was happening around us.

Closing out my email account, I gathered my dishes and walked to the sink to rinse off the residue and threw them in the dishwasher. Climbing the stairs, MaKenzie flashed through my mind and I smiled. I missed her feisty ass, but I knew the reunion between us was going to be tough. Our courtship, that's what I called it, was decent. She pulled away when everything happened with her grand-mother.

Many used to question why I fucked with her so heavy, but it wasn't their business and I didn't give them much to go on. There was a lot of speculation and no validation to what we actually had going on. She was my heavy hitta and I treated her as such, but Makenzie knew how much she meant to me. It was that damn Storm that put up a wall and ignored my ass for the past two years.

No matter how many times I called for her to come back to work, she wasn't trying to hear me. When I found out what was going on in Chicago with her people, I was mad as hell because she could've been making money doing what she opted to do for the love of family. The shit just didn't make sense to me, but I let her do what she thought was best for her.

Leaving my home about an hour later, I jumped in my 2020 Range Rover and hit the road to Club Heat. I was anxious to see my girls and to see how they would react to the changes of the team. So much had changed since they'd been inactive. Hopefully, everything will work out because I needed the team to be solid again, and the twins were a major part of that.

Chapter 4

MaKenzie

I'm a savage, attitude nasty
Talk big shit but my bank account match it
Hood, but I'm classy, rich but I'm ratchet
Haters kept my name in they mouth, now they gaggin'
Bougie, he say the way that thang move it's a movie
I told that boy, we gotta keep it low leave me the room key
I done bled the bloc and now it's hot
Bitch, I'm Tunechi, a mood and I'm moody

Megan Thee Stallion and Beyoncé's "Savage" remix was my new anthem. Cruising to Club Heat, I rapped hard as hell while flexin' in my drop top Benz. Couldn't nobody tell me shit even if they tried, a bitch felt good than a muthafucka. I decided to wear my natural hair and I had straightened it bone straight.

The black leather halter shirt hugged my girls just right and re-vealed the diamond pistol belly ring I was sporting. I had on a pair of black leather jeggings that hugged my cheeks to perfection. The mint green Louboutins that blessed my feet showed off the pedicure I had gotten before leaving Boston.

Pulling into the parking lot of the club, MaKayla stepped out of her green Camaro, looking just like me. I swear her ass got a camera in my shit because there's no way she dressed like me on instinct. We're twins, but I didn't think that's how the shit worked. She had on the exact same outfit except her shoes were a darker green.

I got out with a frown on my face and Kayla laughed. She al-ready knew I was lowkey mad because she was always stealing my style. We were some bad bitches regardless and she was lucky we were sisters.

"Kayla, why the fuck—"

"Shut up, you don't like it, go in your trunk. I'm quite sure you have a hoe bag back there, change."

"Why can't you change? I worked hard on this look," I snapped.

"I can't change because I have a whole man. There's no need for me to have a hoe bag."

"Correction, you had a man. Conte said he wouldn't be there when you got back, remember?" I laughed.

I knew the statement was too soon and regretted saying it the minute it left my mouth. Kayla made the decision to leave Chicago despite how Conte felt, but she wasn't happy about it. My sister loved that man, but one thing we have never done was allow anyone to dictate what we do with our lives. If Conte hadn't given her an ultimatum, I think he would've had a better chance of Kayla staying there with him.

"Sis, I'm sorry. I shouldn't have said that." I tried to clean shit up, but my sister rolled her eyes and walked toward the door with purse in hand. Snatching my own purse from the floor of my car, I hurried to catch up with her as she rang the bell to get inside.

Kayla was upset, because she didn't turn around at all when I stood behind her. My attention went to the person that walked to the door to allow us entry. Summer was still walking around Club Heat like she was that bitch. She deemed to be the queen but was nothing more than a peasant. The look on her face said a thousand words as she realized who was waiting to get in that bitch.

Summer unlocked the door and rolled her eyes, at me in particular. She didn't fuck with me, but I fucked with her mental every chance I got. That day wasn't about her, so I was going to let her be great for a moment, because she was gonna be sick when her nigga started sniffing up my ass.

"Hey, Kayla," Summer said, trying to lean in for a hug.

Kayla stepped back and put her hand up to halt that shit. "You don't fuck with my sister. Therefore, I don't fuck with you. We don't do that fake shit around these parts. Where's Heat?"

Summer looked shitty as hell as she pointed toward the back of the club. MaKayla and I strolled away from her like two supermodels. Glancing down at my watch, I noticed we were almost thirty minutes late as we approached the door to the conference room. Knocking on the door three times, we waited until Heat called out for us to come in.

When we entered, all eyes turned in our direction. I scanned the room and noticed a lot of muthafuckas were missing. There were about three niggas from the originals sitting in the room, and about twelve I didn't know from a can of paint. Heat knew I didn't play well with folks I didn't know. Usually, I would be in the loop of any changes, but I guess since I was away, he didn't feel the need to make me aware of what was going on in the business.

"Damn, Heat, you didn't tell us you had bitches coming through," a nigga called out, looking like he was rescued off the corner shaking a red plastic cup for change.

"Hold that shit down, Loco," Heat said, trying to defuse the situation.

"These bitches fly as fuck! Is this the new entertainment? We can use a set of fine ass twins swinging from the pole in the strip club!"

"Loco, enough!" Heat said louder than before, but dude had put his foot in his mouth already.

"Oh, don't shut him up, Heat. Let that nigga continue to show his Cirque Du Soleil, because he's looking like a real clown right now," I chuckled with a hint of fire in my eyes.

Dreux peeped what was going on and he jumped from his seat, but he wasn't fast enough. Before he could make it across the room to where I was, I had already upped my pistol and had it pointed at Loco's head. The entire room got silent.

"Come on, Storm, it don't call for all this. He didn't know," Dreux said, pleading with his eyes. He knew not to touch me when I was in that mode. "Bossman was waiting until you and Kane arrived to say anything about y'all. Put the gun away."

"Nigga, don't ever speak on my name when you don't know shit!" I sneered, digging the nozzle into his temple.

"You must've never been taught not to pull a pistol unless you're ready to use it," Loco smirked.

"Oh, I can definitely use this bitch. She's the best on my team," I said, cocking my piece, putting a bullet in the chamber.

"Storm! Put that shit down and take a seat. This shit is not part of the reason I called this meeting. Y'all been gone damn near two years and shit hasn't changed. You still a hothead and you have to work on that, man. I've been telling you this for the longest time."

We locked eyes and I backed up. "It doesn't matter how long I've been gone. I'm the same muthafucka that left this bitch. The same person you molded me to be. Act like you know," I snapped, placing my tool back in my bag.

"Fill us in, Heat. Who is these—"

"You better watch ya tongue, fam. Don't let the bitch word fall from your lips when addressing us." Kayla stepped in before I could.

"Kane, I got this. Have a seat," Heat said, standing to his feet. "A few things have changed upon your absence. We lost a couple of the old hittas and gained a few new ones. I want the two of you to meet Loco, whom you've already met."

"Fuck Loco. He has already proven he's bitch made, and I don't like his ass," I said, crossing my legs like the hardcore diva I was born to be.

"Fuck you too! This is a man's game, why the hell do you have females in this muthafucka anyway, Heat?"

"We're here because we are the best in this muthafucka! Keep talking shit and you shall soon find out firsthand," I said, grilling his ass without blinking. "Don't write a check yo' ass can't cash and that's on me, baby."

"Storm! We ain't about to go through this shit, okay? This ain't the time for you to throw shots at anybody," Heat said angrily.

"Throw shots? This nigga is referring to me in a fucked-up manner! Since when have I ever sat back and let a muthafucka judge me by appearance? Not never! And I won't start today. You better share my credentials with his ass, before he come up missing!"

"Pipe that shit down, ma. We're all here to work together. We not the enemy."

I glanced to my right to see who was talking and the nigga that stood up was fine as fuck. His caramel complexion glistened in the sunlight that shined through the window. When the light hit his eyes, they were gray and beautiful. The tattoos displayed on his arms were sexy and I kind of wanted to know the story behind each one. His biceps looked like he hit the gym twice or more a day.

My eyes traveled down his body and his abs were so strong, I could see them ripple through his black tee. His legs were bowed, and I knew right off bat he had a stick that was thicker than a two by four. Obviously, he had on boxers and not briefs in the gray joggers he was sporting. His calves were strong as hell and he had big feet. Admiring him from head to toe didn't stop me from popping off on his ass too.

"Far as I'm concerned, all you muthafuckas are enemies except Big Will, Rocko, and Dreux. I don't know shit about none of y'all. Who are you anyway?"

"I'm Phantom and I'm not about to sit here and let you talk greasy to me. It's uncalled for and I'm trying to have the utmost respect for you. That mouth gon' get you in trouble one of these days. I hope you're as good as you portray yourself to be, you gon' need all your skills in this game."

"Phantom, huh? I'm true to this, I ain't never new to this. I hear what you're saying and I'll try to keep it trill with you. But I meant what I said about ya boy, fuck him! Continue, Heat."

Heat looked at me like he wanted to slap the shit out of me, but I wasn't worried about his ass either. He knew what the fuck I was about and he needed to let that shit be known. Loco shook his head as he bit his lip, I guess he was trying to stop himself from saying anything else to me.

"Like I was saying before I was rudely interrupted. There are some new faces on the team. We got Loco, Phantom, Killah, Haze, and Khaos." I stopped listening as Heat introduced the other new members of the team because they looked weak as hell to me.

"We got off to a rocky start today, but I want everybody to squash all that shit that happened a few minutes ago. This ain't that type of party," Heat said, glancing around the room.

"Heat, I don't mean no disrespect, but I want to say something," Kayla said, rising to her feet. "My sister and I have been on this team for a while now. We will not be addressed as bitches, hoes, or thots. We can hang with the best of them when it comes to going out to get at a mark. Y'all shoot, we shoot, y'all fight, we fight, y'all got our backs, we for damn sure got yours. But the minute either one of us smell bullshit, we puttin' an end to that shit and we don't give a fuck who's on the receiving end. Long as that's understood, I will make sure there's no more problems out of my sister."

Kayla was staring directly at Loco when she spoke her peace. Like me, she didn't give a fuck who was behind the venom she was spitting. That's the way our brother Scony taught us to be. We didn't back down from nobody at any given time.

"Kane, your words were heard loud and clear. Can I get back to what I was saying so we can get outta here?" Heat asked sarcastically. Kayla nodded her head and sat back down and crossed her arms over her chest.

"We lost a slew of veterans on the job and we won't allow that to happen again. When you are given an assignment, there will always be two or more people on that job. We have to watch each other's backs at all times. So whatever beef you have, deal with that shit to the best of your ability *before* you go out on my mission."

There were a lot of heads nodding, acknowledging what Heat had said. I had every intention to holla at Loco about his mouth so we would have a clear understanding from that point on. As I listened to Heat, I could feel somebody looking directly at me. Trying to ignore the feeling, I looked up and Phantom was watching me with his bottom lip between his teeth.

"We will meet back here Sunday and I will give everybody their assignments. Storm," he said sternly. I snatched my attention away from Phantom and gave it to Heat. Jealousy showed on his face, but he already knew what we had was a distant memory.

"Yes." I smiled because he was pissed because he caught me eye fuckin' Phantom.

"Where is Tornado?"

"I tried calling her and she hasn't responded. Maybe you should try calling her. It's obvious she's ignoring my calls."

"I'll get at her but whatever y'all got going on, dead that shit!" Heat's voice boomed through the room.

"For your information, we haven't fallen out or anything. Where the hell did that come from? You know something I don't?" I was confused as hell by Heat's rebuttal. Nicassy and I hadn't said three words to each other since I saw her at the hospital when Poetry was having her baby, and that was damn near a year prior.

"Well, something is wrong if she's not answering for you."

"Heat, she's not answering for me either and I know for a fact there haven't been any malicious words exchanged between the two of us. So, I'm with Storm on this one. We're clueless," Kayla said, rolling her eyes.

"I'll find out what the problem is. Until then, I want y'all back here at one o'clock Sunday afternoon. Meeting adjourned. Storm, I need to talk to you."

Heat turned his back staring out the window. Kayla threw her purse over her shoulder and walked over to where I was standing. "I'm going home to take a nap. Call me later because I want to hit the club. This muthafucka be jumping and we in here tonight."

"I'm down. I'll hit you up later. I'm going home to do the same, since you're deciding to drag me into these Atlanta streets. Let me see what Heat wants and I'll text you when I'm on my way home."

"Okay, sis. I love you and don't lose your cool any more today."

"I hear you, but I can't make any promises." Hugging my sister, I waited for the last person to leave the conference room and sat down in the chair facing the direction Heat was standing. "You just gon' stand there like you didn't tell me you wanted to talk?"

Heat spun around, stalked over to where I was sitting and hovered over my head. "What the fuck was all that shit you were doing?"

"I know damn well you're not coming at me over some shit another nigga started from the gate! Loco shot off at the mouth soon as we walked into the room and I was ready to show him what crazy truly looked like. Get out my face with all that and check that nigga."

"MaKenzie, you know muthafuckin' well I'm not talking about that shit between you and Loco! What was all that lusting shit you were doing with Phantom?"

41

"Seriously, Romero. I'm MaKenzie now?" I chuckled. "I stopped fuckin' around with you before *anything* ever happened with my grandmother. How are you in my face on a jealous rampage, when there's nothing between us? We are done. I don't have to explain nothing I do to you. This is the way you wanted it and I've only followed through. Get out ya feelings."

"You are off limits to anybody on this team—"

"Says the nigga that fucked his business manager and probably still is. Gone with all that rah-rah because Kenzie is going to do whatever she feels fit. There's nothing you would ever be able to tell me. I'm single and ready to mingle. Whoever I'm giving pussy to, isn't a concern of yours," I said truthfully.

"I have never fucked her, and I don't know how many times I've told you that. Stay away from Phantom!"

He was serious as hell but wasn't moving shit my way. When Heat told me he needed time, that's exactly what I planned to give him, then my grandmother passed away. I hadn't thought of him in any way, other than being the nigga I worked with. Now, the minute I pop back up on the scene, he wanted to stake claim. Nah, that shit was dead. Before I could say anything to his foolery, there was a knock on the door, then it opened.

Not bothering to see who had entered, I kept my eyes on Heat and he stood up to his full height and backed away from me. Curiosity got the best of me and I had to see what made him change his demeanor. Summer stood in the doorway glancing back and forth between us and I smiled as I grabbed my purse and stood.

"Is she the reason you didn't come home last night?" Summer asked.

"Don't come in here with this shit, Summer. I'm in a meeting and you're interrupting business."

"But you want to dictate what the fuck I do," I laughed. "Stay out my business, Romero. Handle your affairs and leave me out of it. Everything seems good on your end. Trying to get back with me will disrupt your life, we're not going to cross that line. Make sure you call Nicassy to see what's up with her. I'll holla at you Sunday."

"Storm!" Heat yelled.

"Fuck you, Heat," I said, walking out of the conference room with Summer's eyes staring daggers in my back. That hoe knew not to say anything to me. She was smart to keep that shit funky with Heat and not me.

Meesha

Chapter 5

MaKayla

As I made my way out of Club Heat, the sun was shining bright and I dug around in my purse to get my sunglasses and ran into what felt like a brick wall. My phone fell from my hand and I was glad I'd purchased the shatterproof case and screen protector for my phone. The last thing I needed was a cracked screen.

"Damn, ma. My bad, I shouldn't have been standing in the doorway."

The unidentifiable man bent down to retrieve my phone and I wanted to reach down and stroke his dreads. Conte's face flashed before my eyes and I had to remember I was in Atlanta on business. When he raised up, he turned with my phone held out and I accepted it swiftly.

"So, what's your name, beautiful?" he asked, smiling. Seeing his face, I recognized him as the dude Khaos from the meeting.

His pearly whites were beautiful. Khaos stood about six foot four and his dark complexion was sexy as hell and didn't have a bump in sight. As a matter of fact, his face looked smoother than a baby's ass. The goatee he sported was crisp and curved just right around his mouth. Diverting my attention away from his face, I pulled my sunglasses out and placed them over my eyes while I admired him on the low.

"Khaos, Heat introduced me inside, how soon must you forget."

"Bossman introduced you as Storm."

"Correction, he said my name was Kane. Storm is my sister. I see we're going to be getting mixed up a lot around here. Look, I gotta go." As I walked around him, he reached out and captured my elbow in his strong grasp.

"Hold on. Why you running off so fast?" Khaos asked, licking his lips. "I want to get to know you."

"I know exactly what that means, and I'm not interested. I have a man at home waiting, so I won't be doing any entertaining while I'm away."

"So, tell me, how he allowed yo' fine ass to leave his sight to murk muthafuckas and he's not by your side?"

"Allow? I don't need anybody to *allow* me to do shit. He knew what it was when he got with me, so what could he do other than sit back and wait for me to come back?" I snapped.

"I didn't mean no harm, baby. I just needed to know, because if you were my woman, you would be at home taking care of home. Not running around tracking niggas down for a dollar. I'd make sure you straight at all times."

"That's the thing, my man holds shit down for the both of us, but I'm just that independent female that don't sit on her ass, waiting for a nigga to wine and dine her. I go out and do what I love and take care of home right next to my nigga. I didn't choose this life. The life chose me and I'm rolling with it. The type of female you're looking for is out there somewhere. She's just not within me."

"Independency is a lovely thing, ma. I'm not knocking that at all. The life we live is a dangerous game. You're too beautiful to be out in these streets thuggin' it out with the big dogs. Not saying you and your sister won't be able to handle what comes with the job, but I'm confused as to why."

"Why what?" I asked with a raised eyebrow.

"Kane," Khaos paused, cracking a smile. "I'm not calling you that shit. I'm trying to holla at you on a personal level and Kane is a nigga's name. What's your real name, love?"

"Hurricane. That's what you will call me because I don't know you. The same way you call yourself Khaos, I call myself Kane. As a reminder, there won't be any getting to know me on a personal level. I got a man, period."

"I'm gon' let you think that. When I got my eye on something, I go full force to get it. You're in the spotlight, beautiful. I'll see you around," he said, taking a step back. "You look nice by the way. Wearing the shit out of them pants. But I won't hold you much longer. Enjoy the rest of your day, Miss Lady."

I waved goodbye and hurried to my car because his deep baritone had my lower region screaming. I hit the unlock button on my key fob and wasted no time hopping in the driver's seat of my car.

Khaos nodded his head in approval to my wheels and I felt my face heating up. I had to stay as far away from him as possible.

Even though Conte and I had words before I left, I still loved him. I couldn't let temptation ruin the little bit of faith, I had in us working things out when I got back to Chicago. I backed out of the parking spot and headed in the direction that would lead me to my home. Stopping at a stoplight, my phone rang, and my brother Scony's name appeared on the radio display. Hitting the talk button on the steering wheel, I smiled.

"Hey, big brother!"

"Don't 'hey big brother' me, Kay! What the fuck are you doing? I thought you was done with that hitman shit." Scony's voice filled the interior of my whip loudly.

"Whoa! Who told you that? Kenzie and I made sure shit was cool before we jumped back into what we do. Where's everybody getting their information that we retired from? Somewhere down the line, shit got twisted because we never told anybody that shit."

"It's been almost two years and y'all was home with family. We've been through enough, Kay. Wouldn't you agree?" My brother lowered his voice and calmed down a little bit.

"We were home because shit kept happening back-to-back. There was no way we would've left y'all like that. We stayed to make sure everything was good and when we got the call, it was time to fly the friendly skies."

"You built a whole relationship and just said fuck it to do you. That was some selfish shit, sis. Did you have any type of consideration for how Conte felt? The love he has for you is undeniable and you basically said fuck him. That's not how you handle someone you claim to love. There are sacrifices to be made when you allow someone in your space. You were wrong for that."

"Scony, I know you're not calling me because Conte told you I went back to work," I said, pulling off from the light and hopping on the expressway. "Bro, I didn't say fuck him. What I did say was I had to come to Atlanta for work. I'm not putting my life on hold for anybody. Do I love Conte? Yes, I do, but what I'm not going to

47

tolerate is anybody giving me an ultimatum. He said he's done, he made a choice."

"And you gon' just walk away from what y'all got?"

"I didn't walk away from shit, Scony. You're worried about ya boy's feelings, what about mine? Did I come crying to you when he said if I left, he was done? Nah, I didn't because that shit weak as fuck! You didn't teach me to go hard so I could bow down to a nigga that's throwing ultimatums in my face."

"Sis, going hard doesn't mean you can't have love. You can lose yourself in this game and you deserve to be loved on all levels. I want you to be happy and you were with Conte. I can't tell you what to do, but I think you need to think about your future. Talk to that man and go home. Leave that street shit alone before you lose what you have. Real talk."

"Scony, you got out of the streets when Jade entered your life. What you did for a living didn't alter the way she felt about you. It worked because she loved you for you. She didn't give you an ultimatum to get out of the drug game, you got out when the time was right. That's not what's going on with me and Conte. He's throwing his testosterone around and wants me to follow his lead. The path he wants to lead me down isn't the way I'm trying to go.

"I move to my own beat, and I love the music I make when I'm on a job. For the record, Atlanta is my home, Chicago is where my family is, there's a difference. Tell Conte, since he got you on speed dial, to call me without his caveman mentality. I'll holla at you later."

Ending the call with my brother, I felt some type of way because he knew better than to call me on behalf of Conte. There was nothing wrong with his hands. He hadn't attempted to call my phone since I left the house. Fuck him. If he wanted to whine to Scony instead of talking to me, so be it.

The rest of the car ride was quiet, and I concentrated on the road all the way home. Hitting the button on the garage opener, I pulled inside and cut the engine. Being back in Atlanta gave me a sense of peace because I felt my granny around me. I walked into my home and flipped the switch to turn the light on in the kitchen.

"Hey, Ladybug. How ya doing?" I said out loud. Whenever I walked into my home, I spoke to my granny because I knew she was there waiting for me. Many who had witnessed it, thought I was crazy at first and always questioned if I was alright. There was no need to explain because it wasn't for them to understand. Dropping my purse on the table, I walked to the sink and washed my hands before opening the fridge to grab the bowl of fruit I prepared earlier after grocery shopping. Popping a piece of cantaloupe in my mouth, I closed my eyes because the chilled melon aroused my taste buds like I knew it would.

As I walked through my home, my heart swelled because I'd accomplished so much here in Atlanta and I was glad to be back. It was just me and nothing was out of place. No clothes on the floor, I wasn't tripping over Timbs, Jordans, or Nike flip-flops. Everything was in its rightful place but there was one thing missing, Conte.

I was used to coming home to his masculine scent. Now the smell that filled my nostrils was the vanilla aroma coming from the Airwick plugin. Climbing the stairs, I checked out all the pictures I had on the wall and smiled because every picture was of my granny. As I walked into my bedroom, I sat the bowl on the nightstand and started stripping off my clothes. Relaxing was what I wanted to do before I hit the club and let my hair down.

Pulling my white "Meesha's Pen Spit Fire" tank over my head, I slipped on a pair of boy shorts and crawled onto my king size bed and grabbed the remote. Remembering I left my purse downstairs, I groaned because I had to get my ass up to get it. I raced downstairs and was back in no time and got comfortable as I started watching *Love at First Sight* on *Netflix*.

After watching the first episode, I started to drift off to sleep. My mind was cloudy and deep down inside, I was hoping Conte would call. Dialing his number was out of the question because I was not going to be the first to reach out. *I wasn't the one to give the ultimatum, was I?* I said in my head and closed my eyes.

Meesha

Chapter 6

Phantom

"Storm is a fine muthafucka! If I would've met her in the streets, I wouldn't have thought she was rough around the edges."

"You better leave that bitch where she at. If I was you, I wouldn't try to deal with her. That attitude tells all you need to know about her disrespectful ass."

I was on my way to drop Loco off at the crib since he hopped in my whip with me for the meeting. Taking my eyes off the road for a spell, I glanced at him and laughed out loud. I had tears clouding my vision because his ass was big mad.

"Nigga, you mad because she didn't shrink down to yo ass like these birdbrain chicks. She's a different breed, man. As far as her attitude, I got something to calm all that shit down. See, she's uptight because she needs dick in her life."

"Phantom, you always think yo' dick can cure anything! That's why you got that stupid bitch Tiffany to deal with for the next twelve years."

"Think? I know my dick is the solution to any female's problem. It's the reason Tiff is doing the most, she ain't getting none," I laughed harder. "I'm gon' get her pretty ass. I just have to figure out how to tell her apart from her sister, both of them look just alike. I would hate to be the nigga fuckin' boffum. That shit don't sound too bad."

"Leave both of their asses alone. Birds of a feather flock together, especially twins. That bitch is crazy as fuck and I have a feeling I'm gon' have to kill her ass."

"Loco, you ain't killing shit. Own up to your shit, you were wrong for calling her out of her name. She upped that thang on your ass and you were ready to shit where you were sitting. That shit was hilarious but serious at the same time. Lil mama wasn't playing witcha. Real shit, you owe her an apology, fam."

"I don't owe her nothing! She gotta earn that shit, on the real."

"In my opinion, she did when she had yo' ass shaking in your shoes," I laughed as I pulled into his driveway.

"Whatever, nigga. You going to Club Heat with us tonight? It's time to turn up before we're sent back out there to murk a muthafucka."

"I wasn't planning on it, but I'll see what's up when I go see Layla. I know where you niggas will be, if I decide to get out, I'll come through."

"Aight, cool," Loco said as he got out of my whip and closed the door.

I backed out of his driveway and headed toward my baby mama's crib. Tiffany was a pain in my ass when it came to me seeing our six-year-old daughter. She tried her best to keep me out of the picture because I didn't want to fuck with her on a sexual level. None of that would ever keep me away from my seed. Long as I took care of her and spent time, I was gon' always be a present factor in her life. All that other bullshit was irrelevant.

Thinking long and hard about calling Tiff to let her know I was on my way, I decided against it and decided to pop up. The closer I got to her crib, the more the pit of my stomach clenched. Something wasn't right and it caused me to put pressure on the gas pedal. I pulled into the empty spot in front of the townhome I paid for monthly and hopped out.

I rang the doorbell and waited for someone to answer when I heard glass shattering on the other side of the door. Racing back to my whip, I grabbed my .380 and went back and took my chance at turning the knob. When I was able to gain access freely, I took that shit. I heard my baby girl screaming and crying from somewhere within the house, so I followed her cries.

"Bitch, I'll kill yo' muthafuckin' ass! You won't ever be in this muthafucka cryin' ova anotha nigga! I'm in here and what I do ain't enough because you too busy reminiscing about yo' punk ass baby daddy!"

"Please, let my mommy go, Butch! Don't hit her again," Layla pleaded.

"Shut the fuck up, go to your fuckin' room where I told yo' lil ass to go earlier!"

The commotion was coming from the kitchen and that's the direction I headed with my tool at my side. I didn't give a fuck what the fuck was going on, but it wasn't going down in front of my daughter. Entering the doorway of the kitchen, Tiff was hemmed up by her nigga of the month and her lip was bleeding. My daughter was grabbing at his shirt, but he continued to ignore her and continued to choke the shit out of her mama.

I crept into the kitchen and grabbed Layla by the arm. She turned around and her eyes lit up like a Christmas tree when she saw me. Putting my finger up to my lips, I motioned for her to leave the kitchen and she did without incident. When she was out of the room, I stalked up to the nigga and placed my tool to his head.

"Let her the fuck go, nigga!" I gritted.

Butch turned around with a scowl on his face. "This my bitch! You in my shit," he said, with one hand still around Tiffany's neck. "Yo' punk ass came over here with a pistol, nigga? Fight me like a man, bitch!"

I didn't need to kill nobody that particular day, so I placed my tool on top of the island and punched his ass square in his nose. Blood gushed out onto his shirt and he charged me full force. I side stepped and shoved his head into the wall, making a huge indentation. Butch was fumbling under his shirt and instinct kicked in and I grabbed my pistol and shot him twice, once in each leg.

"Noooooo! Why did you shoot him?" Tiffany's stupid ass screamed. "Stop standing there and call nine-one-one!"

"I don't fuck with twelve, you call them muthafuckas. I'm taking my baby and I'm out."

"You not taking her anywhere, Phantom!" Tiffany said, running up behind me as I walked out of the kitchen. "Yo' ass going to jail for what the fuck you just did!"

"Tiff, you sound stupid. Look at your face, man! That nigga was in here whooping yo' ass and you trying to protect him! Go in there and get his busta ass some help before he die on yo' goofy ass," I said, walking down the hall. "Layla, let's go, baby."

Layla appeared in the doorway of her bedroom with tears running down her face. Tiffany was still behind me, trying to push past me. Blocking her by placing my arm on the wall, I motioned for Layla to come to me. She moved slowly in my direction with her hand in her mouth.

"Take your ass back in that room right now, Lay!"

"Holla at her again! Go in there with the nigga that was whoopin' on your stupid ass. Come on, Layla, so we can get out of here."

As I held my daughter's hand, her mama kept punching me in my back, but I didn't stop to address that shit because it didn't faze me. When she tried to snatch my daughter by her arm, that's when I wanted to knock her head off. My temperature went up several degrees as I glared at her.

"Get the fuck on, Tiff. I'm tired of your shit," I said simply, pushing her back.

"You put yo' hands on me! That's called assault and you going to jail for that too!"

I couldn't do nothing but laugh because I pushed her and she was ready to snap, but Butch literally whooped her ass and gave her gifts to show off and I'm going to jail. That's the stupid shit these females be on and I wanted no parts of it. Prying my daughter out of her grasp, we were able to leave out the door. Opening the back door of my midnight black Benz for my princess, I waited for her to get inside and made sure she was buckled safely in the seatbelt before closing the door. As I got in the driver's seat, I glanced in the rearview mirror at Layla.

"Talk to me, baby," I said, backing out of the spot.

"I heard a gunshot. Did you kill him, Daddy?"

"Nah, he will live. You don't have nothing to worry about."

"You should've killed him," she said lowly, but I heard her loud and clear.

"Why?" I asked curiously.

Layla was sitting quietly with her head down. I didn't rush her to tell me what she meant, I just continued to drive. Ten minutes passed before her tiny voice was heard again.

"Butch always hits my mama after he smokes that stinky stuff. He starts sweating and his eyes get really big. When Mama tells him to stop or get out, that's when he starts hitting her."

"Does he hit you, Layla?" I asked, slowing the car down in case I needed to pop a U-turn and head back to finish the job.

"No, he just yells at me and tells me to go in my room. I don't like him though. Butch is going to hurt my mama one day. That's why I wish you would've killed him. I don't want to live there anymore, Daddy. I'm scared to go to sleep at night."

"You have nothing to worry about, baby. I'm going to do everything I can so you can live with me. It's going to take time. For now, it's me and you for the weekend. How does that sound?" I asked with a smile.

"I'm happy. I love you, Daddy."

"I love you too, baby girl. What do you want to eat?"

"Tacos!" she yelled excitedly.

"Tacos it is," I said, heading to her favorite taco spot.

***

We got Layla's tacos and I headed to the expressway to go home. Layla was singing along to H.E.R. and I listened with a smile, because my baby was singing her little heart out. She sounded good too. I had to research some vocal classes because she got something special with that voice.

"Daddy, can I go to Grandma Karla's house?"

"What? Layla, I thought it was going to be me and you this weekend," I said in my sad voice.

"Daddy, don't be sad. We can hang out tomorrow. please?"

Reaching down into the cupholder, I grabbed my phone and dialed my mama up. Without waiting for her to answer, I handed Layla the phone and continued to drive. I took the exit to my mama's house because she never told her only grandchild no under any circumstances.

"Heyyyy, Grandma! I'm with my daddy and I want to come to your house, can I?" Layla asked, putting the call on speaker.

"You know Granny's baby can come over. I've missed you, Lay Lay."

"Miss you too. My daddy is sad because I wanted to come spend time with you."

"Oh, he will get over it. Xavier, how long is it going to take you to get here?" my mama asked.

"Come on the porch, old lady," I said, pulling into her driveway. Soon as I stopped the car, Layla was taking her seatbelt off and opened the door. "I guess I'll be eating your tacos since you left them in the back seat. And come back with my damn phone."

My daughter wasn't trying to hear me. My mama was standing on the porch with her arms outstretched and Layla ran right into them. The relationship the two of them had was amazing and I loved it.

"Can I get some of that love?" I said after retrieving my daughter's food from the car.

"You've gotten my love for twenty-seven years, boy. I know you're not still jealous of your own child."

My mother laughed as she and Layla went inside the house, leaving me to fend for myself. I walked inside and locked the door. I could hear my daughter telling my mother about what happened at her mother's house and I wanted to kick my own ass for not making it clear to not tell grandma.

"Xavier! You shot somebody while my baby was in that house?"

"Ma, the nigga was reaching for a pistol, so I had no choice but to get at him before he got me," I said, walking into the living room.

"Did you kill him?" she asked.

"No, Grandma. He didn't kill him, but he should've. Butch hits my mama all the time."

Layla was telling everything, and my mama was looking upside my head like I was at fault. I guess my baby was trying to ensure she wouldn't have to go back to Tiffany's house. But she was throwing me under the bus at the moment.

"Ma, I did what I had to do. I walked in and he was choking the hell out of Tiff and couldn't let that ride. I put my tool down to beat the fuck out of him but when I knocked his ass out, he started fumbling under his shirt and I shot his ass."

"I'm not worried 'bout you shooting him per se, what scares me is the fact this isn't over. He's going to come after you, Xavier."

"Ma, I'm not worried about none of that. If it happens, be ready to hold Layla down, because I'm going to jail." Layla looked up at me and tears welled in her eyes. "Come here, baby." She jumped into my arms and buried her face in my neck. "Daddy gon' be alright. I'm not going anywhere, okay?"

Without answering, she nodded her head yes and I put her down. Handing her the bag of food, she raced to the kitchen table and started eating the tacos she so desperately wanted. My mama was very quiet and that prompted me to sit next to her on the couch. I put my arm around her shoulders and brought her in for a hug.

"Ma, you don't have anything to worry about. Nothing's going to happen to me. Butch ain't on shit."

"Stop all that cussing in my house! I let it slide the first couple times, but you getting carried away now. Just be careful, baby. You're all I got and I don't know if I would be able to live another day if you weren't here on earth with me."

"God ain't ready for me just yet. We not gon' dwell on that," I said, kissing her forehead.

"I'm gon' keep Layla for the night. Go out and have some fun, son."

"Nah, you don't have to do that. Going out is not a priority over my daughter."

"Get out and go party. I know there's somewhere you can go. You ain't gotta go home, but you gotta get the hell outta here. This time is about to be about me and my grandbaby. Don't worry about bringing any clothes, she has everything she needs here."

"Aight, I'm out. Layla, give me a kiss. I'm about to go."

Layla put her taco down and raced over to where I stood. "I love you, Daddy. Me and Granny is about to turn up!" she screamed, dancing in front of me. Hugging me around my waist, I bent down and kissed her cheek.

"I love you too, baby. I'll see you tomorrow."

Leaving out of my mother's house, I thought about what she said about Butch retaliating. I wasn't worried about him coming for me at all, but I surely would be ready if he did. As I drove to the crib, my phone started ringing and it was Tiffany. There was nothing she could say to me. I let the phone ring to voicemail, and she called right back.

"What, man?" I sneered into the phone.

"Bring my damn baby, Phantom! You were wrong for what you did to Butch!"

"Tiff, you sound stupid as fuck right now. How you defending a nigga that whoops yo' ass on a regular? To make the shit even worse, he kicks yo' ass in front of my daughter!"

"That's not your business! Don't worry about what goes on in my house. Just bring my baby home!" Tiff screamed.

"I'm not bringing her back to that muthafucka, man. I'm going to fight for custody, because yo' crib isn't safe for my seed. The environment is not a place for her to be. She's better off with me."

"If you don't bring me my baby, your life is going to go from sugar to shit faster than lightning. You should've killed Butch, nigga. I can't tell you when, but he's coming for your ass soon as he is healed."

"Keep yo' threats to yo'self, Tiff, before I forget you're the mother of my child. If that nigga come my way, he won't make it to the hospital next time. You better watch what that nigga smoking and make sure it ain't crack. He won't get the chance to raise his voice at my daughter ever in life. As a matter of fact, since your man is so bad ass, he can cover all expenses in yo' muthafuckin' house. I will no longer foot the bill since my daughter won't be there."

"Fuck you, nigga! Bring my child home."

I hung up on her ass and signaled to exit the expressway. Tiffany kept blowing my phone up, but I refused to answer because I didn't have time for her bullshit. Entering my crib, I threw my keys on the table by the door and went straight to the kitchen to warm up my steak burrito. I glanced at the time on the microwave and it was a little after eight o'clock.

The burrito was hitting and I enjoyed it, despite Tiffany calling my phone back-to-back. After throwing my trash away, I headed upstairs to my bedroom and collapsed on the bed. I was sleep within minutes. A nigga was tired as hell and rest was what I needed.

Meesha

Chapter 7

Khaos

Driving up to the valet outside of Club Heat, the line was wrapped around the building and I already knew the night was about to be one for the books. There were quite a few fine ass women that were ready to party, but I didn't want to see none of them. Kane was the only woman I'd been thinking about since I laid eyes on her earlier that day. I should've tried to get her number but hell, she didn't even tell me her real name.

As I climbed out of my gray 812 Superfast Ferrari two-seater, all eyes were trained on me. My locs were freshly twisted and I was sporting a simple black Balenciaga tee with the black pants to match. The black Balenciaga sneakers I had on were fresh out the box and I topped the outfit off with ice on my neck, wrist, and in my ears. The thirst was real as I made my way to the entrance of the club.

"Heyyy, Khaos!" a female called out like I was a celebrity. I waved my hand without turning and kept it moving.

Dapping up the guard at the door, I walked inside, and the music was on point. The DJ was spinning MO3's "Everybody"

Everybody ain't yo' friend
Everybody ain't yo' patna
Everybody ain't no real nigga
If I say I got you, I got you
When it's fucked up and get fucked up
Just hold it down and keep it silent
And when you're not around
I protect yo' name
I won't let a nigga talk about ya

That joint spoke nothing but truth and I fucked with it. Nodding my head to the beat, I made my way to the VIP section that was reserved for our team. Loco, Killah, and Haze was already poppin' bottles and the blunts were in rotation. I looked around and noticed

Phantom wasn't in the building. Usually his ass would beat us to the club.

Walking over to Loco, I sat next to him and whispered in his ear, "Did you tell Phantom we were coming out like I told you to?"

"Yeah, he went to see Layla earlier and said he would see if he would be able to make it," Loco said loudly so I could hear him over the music.

Acknowledging what he said by nodding, I grabbed a bottle of Heineken and used the bottle opener on my keyring to open it. These niggas never wasted time getting hoes to party in our section. There wasn't anything wrong with it, but they chose the most ghetto, money-hungry hoes they could find to join us. Didn't nobody want that type of vibe around, at least I didn't.

"Hi, handsome," a random said, sitting too close to me. She started running her hand up and down my arm and I politely removed her shit. A frown formed on her lips, but she switched up fast as hell and smiled.

"What's up," I said, moving over a little bit.

"Come dance with me."

"I'm cool. I don't dance," I said nonchalantly without giving it a second thought. Waving one of the barmaids over, I placed an order for myself. "Let me get a fifth of Dussé, Brittany." I leaned over and got my money out of my pocket and peeled off a bill, handing it to her.

Ole girl's eyes bulged out of her head as she focused on the knot in my hand. I saw that shit out of my peripheral and laughed to myself. I could only imagine what was going through her thot ass brain, but that shit would never work with a nigga like me. There was no doubt she was gon' try to pull some goofy shit.

Brittany was back within minutes with my bottle and a few glasses. She arranged my items on the table in front of me and held her hand out with my change. Nah, you good," I said, peeling off another forty and gave her that as a tip too. Thirsty Tina reached forward to help herself to my drink and I all but slapped her hand down.

"What the fuck you doing, shawty?"

"I'm getting me a drink," she said, rolling her neck.

"Not over here you not. All that shit over there," I said, pointing to the drinks Loco or whoever bought on the other side of the section. "I don't share drinks with nobody."

"You got a fucked-up attitude anyway. That's why you over here by yourself." She got up and stomped to the table I directed her to and poured her a glass of Cîroc, while giving me the evil eye. I poured myself a drink and proceeded to roll up.

Sitting back against the cushions of the couch, I was vibing by myself as everybody around me was damn near having an orgy. All I could do was shake my head at the bullshit that was taking place. Movement caught my eye from the stairway and my nigga came pimpin' into the section. The same hoes that were on my niggas' dicks, hopped up like they were caught with their hands in the cookie jar.

Phantom looked in my direction and laughed heartily because he already knew what the fuck was up. Standing to my feet, I met him halfway and we dapped up. Passing the wood to him, he pulled on that shit and let the smoke out through his nose.

"You late, nigga!" I said, sitting back down.

"Man, I had a day for the books. I had to bust a cap in Tiff's nigga's ass when I left the meeting. I walked in on that nigga beating her ass. He wanted to square up and I knocked his ass out. He reached for his tool and got two hot ones in the ass."

"You killed that nigga, right?" I asked, sitting up.

"Nah, so I know he bringing heat my way. I couldn't off him because Layla was there. She don't want to go back to that muthafucka, fam. Tiff been blowing my shit up all day throwing threats and shit."

"That's fucked up. My niece with Auntie?"

"Yeah, she bailed on me when ma told her she could stay. That's the only reason I'm out," Phantom said, taking in what was going on in the section. He was looking around slowly like he was looking for somebody. Loco's voice snapped his head in that direction.

"What the fuck they doing here?" Joining us as we all turned toward the stairs.

Storm and Kane were walking up the stairs slowly and all eyes were on them. They were dressed to impress, and both were drop-dead gorgeous. I didn't know which was which but both of them could get the business. One had on a pink linen pantsuit, with a pair of darker-pink heeled sandals that showed off her pretty feet. The other had on a white sheer skirt, with a split that traveled up to her waist. The sheer halter shirt showcased her abs and the black bra underneath. Her pedicure was on point in her six-inch stiletto sandals too.

"Man, Loco. Don't start that shit. They're part of the crew, if you like it or not. We are here to have a good time." I gave him a warning he ignored and kept going with his rant.

"Fuck that! This our section," he said, sounding like a bitch. "They not welcomed up here."

"Says who? What I'm gon' need you to do is take the bitch out-cha voice. That's what you sound like right now. Go over there and get one of them bum bitches since you don't know how to act around royalty, nigga," Phantom said seriously.

Loco didn't move. Instead, he continued to grill Storm and Kane as they made their way over to where Phantom and I were seated. We both stood to our feet and waited until they were close enough for us to speak to them.

"What's up, fellas?" the twin in the pink said smoothly as she looked around the section with her nose turned up. "What the fuck y'all got going on up here?"

"Storm, we are here to have a good time. Don't do that," Phantom said nicely.

"I didn't even say anything," Storm said, looking at Phantom crazy. "If we're going to work together, you have to find a way to tell us apart," she and Kane laughed.

"Okay, so you're Storm?" he asked, pointing to the twin in the white.

"Yep," she said, chuckling.

"And you are Kane?" She nodded her head yeah. "Aight, well, I have my pick of the night," Phantom said, wrapping his arm around Storm's shoulder.

Kane glanced in my direction and sat down on the opposite side of the couch than where I was sitting. Storm looked around and locked eyes with Loco. He sneered before taking a sip of his drink.

"I see y'all boy still in his feelings. I'm gon' need one of you to holla at him before he gets fucked up," Storm said loud enough for both me and Phantom to hear.

"He's cool. You won't have no problems."

"It's not my problem I'm worried about. I'm more concerned for his, to be honest."

"Bring yo' thuggish ass over here and sit down and have a drink with me. You smoke?" he asked, holding the blunt out to her.

"I do, but the only pre-rolls I smoke are the ones I bring to the table. Thanks though," Storm said, going in her purse.

She came out with a spiff that she flamed up between her long snow-white nails. I left Phantom to her and gave my attention to Kane's sexy ass. Picking up my glass, I took a sip before conjuring up a conversation.

"You want something to drink? I got Dussé."

"Thanks, but no thanks. I'm a tequila type of woman," she said, waving to get the barmaid's attention. "Can I get a fifth of Coconut 1800, two glasses of pineapple juice, water and two empty glasses?" she asked, soon as Brittany came over.

Before she could come out of her purse, I had paid for her drink already. When she looked up, there was confusion on her face. "Where did she go? I have to give her the money."

"I took care of it," I said, sipping my drink.

"That wasn't necessary, Khaos," Kane said trying to hand me the money she held in her hand. Shaking my head, she pouted and put it back in her purse.

"I'll let you pay when we go out to dinner. How does that sound?"

"We've been through this already. We won't be getting to know one another, because—"

"You got a man," I said, finishing her sentence. "I heard you say that earlier, but ya man ain't here, is he? There's nothing wrong with having friends, Kane."

"Ain't shit friendly about how you see me," she laughed. "That shit work on bitches like them," she said, motioning around the room. "Not boss bitches."

Kane had a point, I had to find another way to win her over. She was another caliber of woman and I had to think that shit over. I wasn't going to push the issue tonight, but I was about to have a good damn time with her sexy ass. Brittany appeared with her drink and she poured a drink for herself and Storm before taking a sip and blazing up a spiff of her own.

We all sat back, having a good time smoking and drinking. After a while, both of the sisters loosened up and started talking a little bit more. The envious stares they were receiving from the chicken heads were ignored on both ends. The two of them actually found the shit quite funny.

Tyga's "Taste" boomed through the speakers and the twins jumped to their feet and fucked the floor up. The way they were moving had both me and Phantom in a trance. Neither one of us danced when we went out, but when niggas started moving in their direction, we both hopped up and shook the floor with them.

"Taste, taste, you can get a taste. Yeah, that's cool, but he ain't like me," I rapped in Kane's ear as she threw that ass into my pelvis. She had quite a few drinks, but she wasn't to the point of being drunk.

"That shit don't work either," she chuckled when she turned to face me. Her eyes diverted behind me and she looked up at me. "You have a hater in attendance. Let me know if a simple dance will cause a bitch to get these hands or not."

I two-stepped until I was facing the direction she was staring and ole girl from earlier was pissed. "You don't have to worry about her. I don't even know who the hell she is and she's just mad because I'm doing everything with you, I wouldn't do with her."

"Well, she's going to be mad for the rest of the night, because I'm going to keep you occupied for that purpose alone," she said, putting her arms around my neck.

Shid, I had no problem with that at all. When the song ended, we went back to the couch and Kane blazed up once again and that shit was sexy as hell to me. The weed she was smoking smelled like berries and it piqued my curiosity.

"What is that tropical shit you smoking?"

"It's called Za, exotic weed. Try it," she said, passing it to me.

I pulled off that shit and it was hitting. That was my first time having anything like that. I usually stuck with my OG and Kush, but I was going to have to cop some of that from Kane. My boys may clown my ass, but I didn't care, that was fie.

Storm came over and reached out for her sister's hand. "Come to the restroom with me."

Kane stood and told me she would be back as she gave me the spiff. I watched her walk away and had to adjust my dick in my pants. Phantom walked over and poured himself a drink. He shook his head as he looked down at the blunt in my hand.

"What the fuck is you smoking? Shit smell like Bubblicious," he laughed.

I took a pull and held that shit in for a few seconds, then blew it out. "This some shit Kane had and it's exotic weed. This shit is the truth. Hit that."

"That shit sound gay and smell like it was made for females. I'll stick with my OG, nigga. The shit you're willing to go through to get some pussy," he laughed.

"I won't be getting with Kane no time soon. She got a man, fam. She standing on that shit too."

"Since when you give a fuck about another nigga? Make her forget about his ass."

"Nah, I'm gon' leave that up to her. I'm not gon' pressure her in no way at all. She's different and I'm gon' respect that shit and just try to be her friend. Maybe it will turn into a friend with benefits type of thing."

"What up, my niggas?" My nigga Monty strolled into the VIP with his hands in the air.

"Damn, fam, where the fuck you been?" Phantom asked, standing up to give him a brotherly hug.

"Married life and fatherhood's a muthafucka. I come out on a need-to basis now. The wife deserves that much respect. I see the ratchets are still flockin'," he laughed. "Khaos, what up?"

I stood to dap Monty up and it was good to see his ass. We go way back to the days when he was hustling hard in the game. My nigga been through a lot in his young life, but he's doing the damn thang. He opened a restaurant and got married on our ass. We rarely saw him around anymore. So, it was good to see him. Loco came over drunk as hell and hugged Monty tight as hell slapping him on the back.

"Long time no see, nigga," he slurred. Monty stepped back and waved his hand back and forth in front of his face. "My bad. I'm having a good time. You know how I do it," Loco said, looking around. "Where the two bougie bitches at?"

"Who he talking about?" Monty asked. Before anyone could answer his question, Storm and Kane was coming back up the stairs.

"Them sidity hoes," Loco angrily said. Monty turned to see who he was referring to and cocked his head at Loco.

"What's your problem with them?"

Something told me Monty knew exactly who the twins were and Loco had fucked up. He should've shut the fuck up about them when we told him to. Alcohol was always his downfall, outside of his smart-ass mouth. But the two together seemed to get him into shit every time.

"They are new to the crew and I don't like them bitches," he said as the ladies walked up.

"Loco, you still hatin' on a couple of females? Dude, give that shit up," Storm said, without noticing Monty's presence. "I thought we squashed this shit earlier, brah," she laughed, walking up on him.

"Kenzie, I got this," Monty said, grabbing her arm. She looked up at him and a smile spread across her face. "Loco, I have nothing but respect for you and we've never had a problem. But if you disrespect my muthafuckin' family again, that's where the problems will lie. You already know how the fuck I get down, nigga."

"That bitch—"

Monty hit his ass in the mouth so hard his head snapped back, and he hit the floor. I pushed Monty back toward the stairs and Phantom went to help Loco up. Everybody in our section crowded around trying to find out what happened. Loco was wobbly on his feet and I knew it was time to go.

"Nigga, I've told you to go easy on the liquor because it always got yo' ass in trouble. Don't test my muthafuckin' gangsta! I bet you think twice about calling another female out her name. Respect my people!"

Monty refused to go down the stairs. He pushed my hands off him and stood at the top of the stairs. "What are you doing here?" Storm asked. "Let's go outside."

"We can talk right here," Monty growled. "I came to spend some time with y'all to make sure everything was good. Scony called and told me y'all was here. Kayla, you need to call Conte."

"I'm not calling him! He is constantly calling everyone but me. That's bitch shit for real. How about y'all stay the fuck outta my business. Not once has anybody asked me what happened. Y'all going off what the fuck he has told y'all. The shit's funny, because every time a different muthafucka come to me with our problems, the further we will part."

"This ain't the time nor place to discuss this. Come to the house tomorrow so we can talk. I'm out of here. Khaos, don't let that nigga do shit to my family. If he come for you, end that muthafucka's life!"

Monty turned and left while Kane went to retrieve her bottle and headed back toward the stairs. Storm looked at me, "I'm sorry that happened. Talk to Loco because I'm not going to put up with his disrespect much longer. My people will be here to bury his ass if Monty makes that call. I'm going to make sure he doesn't, but Loco needs to understand he's coming for the wrong females."

"Phantom is talking to him now," I said, glancing across the room.

"Would you go tell Phantom to come here a minute? We're about to head out."

I went to get him and he left Loco sitting in a chair as he came to see what Storm wanted. She said something to him and handed him something before hugging him around the neck. Kane stood quietly waiting on her sister and if she was a cartoon character, the steam would be seen coming out of her nose.

Hearing Monty talk about her problems pissed her off and *her man* fucked up by going to everybody but her. I got happy on the inside because there was a chance for me to get to know her on a personal level. I just had to play my cards right. The time would present itself very soon.

Chapter 8

Heat

I was sitting at home in my office checking out everything that was happening in the VIP section of the club. Specifically, the section my team was in. My blood boiled when I saw how much attention Kenzie was giving Phantom after I told her to stay the fuck away from him. I meant what the fuck I said, and she wanted to play with a nigga.

Loco must've said or done something that got his ass laid the fuck out. I couldn't call security fast enough because the nigga left the club right after. That muthafuckin' Loco was going to have to be put on limited alcohol. He was going to end up getting himself killed.

Not long after, I saw Kenzie and Kane leave the club and I jumped up and headed for the door. Hopping in my ride, I made my way to Kenzie's house. She was going to be pissed because I showed up without notice, but I didn't care. She was about to take me serious once and for all.

Her car wasn't in the driveway and I knew she hadn't made it home yet, because the house was dark. Parking two houses away, I had a clear view of her house and would be able to see when she pulled in. I sat for about ten minutes before a pair of headlights appeared from the other end of the street. Soon as she pulled into the driveway, I didn't bother turning on my lights as I pulled in behind her. Getting out of my whip quickly, I made my way to her driver's door and snatched it open. I was met with her tool aimed at my chest.

"You must be ready to die, Heat! Why would you roll up on me like that?" Kenzie screeched, lowering her weapon. She got out of her vehicle and hit the locks as she made her way to the front door. Kenzie unlocked the door and disarmed the alarm, then slammed her purse and keys on the table. She turned toward me quickly with her hands on her hips.

"You got five minutes to get whatever off your chest. Then you can get the fuck out."

"What did I tell you to do?" I asked.

"I don't know. Elaborate on what you're talking about."

"Phantom. I told you to stay away from him, right?"

"First of all, no one tells me what the hell to do! Secondly, who the fuck is you, my father? Let me make this very clear to you, Heat. You have your life and I have mine. We're not together because that's what you wanted. Time away from you made it easier to get you out of my system. If I wanted to start a relationship with your cousin, there would be nothing you could do about it. For the last time, stay out of my business!"

"Kenzie—"

"Stop calling me that! This is a business relationship and from this point on, you will address me as Storm. We are not on a personal level and never will be again."

"That's what your mouth says, *Kenzie*. I made you and you not shit without me."

"Are you insinuating I can't make money without you? Better yet, are you calling yourself threatening me?"

"That's exactly what I'm saying and you know I don't make threats, nothing but promises." I smirked.

"You got your people mixed up. That shit don't move me. I wish you would try to fuck up my money. I'll shoot yo' ass myself, nigga. This is some hoe shit you on. All because I won't fuck with you anymore. For the record, you didn't make me shit! I learned everything I know before I saved yo' ass in your office that day. Did you enhance what I already knew? Absolutely. But made me? You outta yo' muthafuckin mind.

"All of this because you would no longer be able to fuck me. Where the fuck is Summer?" she asked, kicking off her heels.

"Don't worry about Summer. We're talking about us right now."

"There is no us, Heat! Just like you can come out your mouth tell me don't worry about yo' bitch, have that same energy and tell yo'self not to worry about me! I'm telling you now, you are gonna be one mad muthafucka trying to keep up with me. Fuck around and I'll send yo' ass a video of the next nigga with his dick down my throat."

I grabbed her ass by the neck and squeezed with all my might. "Stop playing with me, MaKenzie! I'll kill yo' ass in here."

Kenzie didn't struggle to get out of my grasp. Hell, the shit didn't seem to faze her at all. She stared me straight in the eyes and that shit kind of shook my ass, to be honest. I gave her neck an extra squeeze and pushed her into the wall. She bounced back and slapped the fuck outta me.

"If you ever put yo' hands on me again, I'll kill yo' ass in a heartbeat. Heat, don't fuck with me because yo' ass could be driving one day, and your brakes would mysteriously stop operating. My name is not Summer. Use that bitch as your human punching bag. Make that your first and last time coming at me like that. Get the fuck out of my house!"

Makenzie pointed to the door and I backed up so I could keep my eyes on her. "If you want me off the team, say that shit now. Otherwise, I'll see you Sunday at one o'clock."

"Stay away from Phantom," I said, before leaving her house.

The entire way to my ride, I thought about ways to disrupt her life, since she thought I was a weak nigga. "Makenzie was going to wish she had listened to my warning," I said to myself as I started my car and backed out of the driveway. I dialed Phantom up and waited for him to answer.

"What up, Bossman?" Phantom said, with music bumping in the background. "Hold on, let me go outside. A few minutes later, he was back. "What's going on?"

"What happened with Loco?" I asked, not wanting to go right into my dilemma with Kenzie.

"He had too much to drink and wanted to disrespect Storm again. Her people were in the building and he got his ass knocked out. I warned him about that shit earlier and he decided to do what he wanted to do. That shit was on him. I tried talking to him but he ain't trying to hear nothing I said."

"I'll talk to him about that, because I told him to lay off the alcohol," I said, while thinking of a way to bring up what I really wanted to discuss. "What's going on with you and Storm?"

"What you mean? Ain't shit going on with us, yet. Why you ask?"

"Storm is off limits. She belongs to me. I don't need to go any further on that, since she didn't fill you in on that information."

Phantom laughed, "You got it, Bossman. I'll keep that in mind, but I won't make any promises. Let the best man win. Is there anything else I can help you with?"

"Nah, just remember what I said." I hung up and felt like a lame nigga after that conversation. Kenzie got me doing shit I'd never thought I would ever do. I pushed the gas and headed to my crib so I could get her ass out of my head.

Chapter 9

Nicassy

"Bae, where you going?"

"I have a lunch date with your sisters. I told you that last night," I said, putting the finishing touch on my makeup. "Stone, you have to listen when I talk to you."

"When did you tell me about this, before or after you sucked the soul out of my body?"

Stone wrapped his arms around my waist and nuzzled his nose against my neck, causing me to giggle like a schoolgirl. I had to think about what he said because he was onto something. I did tell him about it after our sex session the night before. He was damn near comatose, so he probably didn't comprehend what I had said.

"Okay, I'll give you that. This pussy had you snoozing like a baby," I laughed.

"Enjoy yourself. How about y'all go to the spa, on me. I'll call ahead and set up the appointment. I'll text the time and location when it's set up."

"Sounds good. Wait before you do anything, you know how your sisters are, always got something to do."

"Send one of those mass texts or something. I'm trying to make sure my baby is relaxed," he said, kissing my cheek.

Doing what he suggested, I sent the text and turned to peck Stone's lips so I could get out of there. "I'll talk to you later, boo."

Leaving the house, I thought about the reason I was in Texas. Ten months ago, I was sent on a job and Heat was adamant about me not telling anyone where I was. That was right up my alley because I needed to get away from everyone anyway. Kenzie wasn't the person I grew to love anymore. She changed somehow and I didn't have the same vibe about her.

Yeah, I was there when shit went down with Scony and the rest of the family, but it seemed like I was an afterthought when it came to the other shit that happened in Atlanta when G found his cousin Kaymee. Then on top of that, Heat was giving her too much attention, like she was Queen of Sheba. So, I distanced myself and took the job soon as it was presented to me.

The only problem I had was the fact that I'd fallen for the fuckin' mark! I hadn't checked in with Heat in the past two months and when I did, I lied my ass off. I'm not trying to kill Stone. He's been too good to me and he is now my man. His family loves me, and I love them. It's been hard keeping my past away from my future. I bought a new phone when things changed and left the old one in my car.

MaKenzie and MaKayla been calling me like crazy and I refused to entertain any conversation with them. I wasn't important to them then, fuck them now. The only regret I had was not keeping in touch with Scony. He was truly like a brother to me and never switched up. He was always there, and I felt bad on so many levels.

Finding a parking spot outside of the restaurant, I put my car in park and got out. As I walked inside, I spotted Celeste and Sam sitting in the back by the window. Strolling in their direction, the two of them were engulfed in a conversation and didn't see me approaching.

"Oh, so y'all started without me, huh?" I said, making my presence known.

"Hey, sis," Sam sang, standing to her feet. "My brother made you late, I see. We haven't ordered yet, but we did get you a drink."

"Something like that," I responded, hugging both of Stone's sisters. "Are y'all available for going to the spa? I have to let your brother know," I asked, sitting down.

"Hell, yeah. Especially if it's free," Celeste said, dancing in her seat.

"I'm down too. I need a day of relaxation," Sam chimed in as I texted Stone and sat my phone on the table.

I had to keep my secret safe because Sam and Celeste really were two cool ass people. They would hate me if they knew the truth of why I had entered their lives. Shaking the thought from my mind, I just wanted to enjoy our time together. I picked up the menu and scanned it to see what I wanted to eat. The waitress approached our table and we all placed our orders.

"How's things been going with y'all?" I asked taking a sip of the sangria they ordered in my absence.

"Girl, Joe muthafuckin' ass is on the verge of getting his ass put the fuck out!" Celeste said, kickin' off the tea.

"Lawd, what the hell has he done now?" Sam asked, rolling her eyes.

Joe was Celeste's on again, off again boyfriend. He'd been giving her the blues since I first stepped on the scene. He was one of them niggas that had community dick available to every woman in Houston. Sis, was always fighting, arguing, or crying over this man. But it wasn't my place to tell her to leave him alone. The only thing I could provide was a shoulder for her to cry on.

"Some bitch called my phone, talking about Joe was her man. Of course, he denied the shit, talking about he didn't know her. I know his ass lying because I don't know her and how the fuck she get my number? The bitch didn't do spin the number to get my shit."

Today was about to be the day I gave her the uncut version of my thoughts. Somebody had to tell her to leave this nigga alone. He was toxic as fuck and she deserved much better.

"How long are you going to let him play with your emotions, Celeste? The warning signs have been going off nonstop since I met you. How much are you willing to take from him? True enough, he provides for you, but it's not like you need him to. You can be on your own and still be good. Stop confusing lust with love, sis."

"I agree with Angel. You don't need that nigga. I want to find his ass and beat the fuck out of him," Sam said angrily. "He has been putting you through this bullshit for the longest time. Move the fuck on from his lying ass, sis. I've tried to be quiet about your relationship, but enough is enough!"

Celeste held her head down and was quiet for a few minutes. It was extremely hard to hear the hardcore truth about somebody you loved, but sometimes the truth was meant to hurt in order to make the right decision. She had been with Joe for years but there was more heartache than sunny days in their relationship. It was time she woke up to see the reality of it all.

"Leaving is easier said than done. Y'all aren't the ones going through this shit. I can't just walk away. I'm pregnant," she whispered.

"Come again?" Sam said, leaning in closer to her sister.

"I'm pregnant. I found out last week and I'm already four months." A tear fell from her eye and I looked under the table so I could see Celeste's stomach and it was still washboard flat.

"Celeste, you don't look pregnant at all. Where the hell is this baby and have you told Joe's hoe ass?" I asked.

Shaking her head no, the tears continued to cascade down her face. Sam was fuming and she had every right to be mad. I would be the same way about my sister if I had one. My phone chimed and Stone texted me the location and time of our spa appointment.

"We have an hour before our appointment. It seems we all need this treatment," I said, after reading the message.

At that time, the waitress came with our food. Sam and I dug in, but Celeste just moved her fork around the plate. I was worried about her. Now that she wasn't keeping her pregnancy to herself, I could see the stress she was really going through.

"Celeste, you don't have to worry about going through this alone. We will be here for you no matter what. Stress is the last thing you need at this time. You have to get yourself together, for the baby at least." I tried to assure her she was not alone, but the tears continued to flow.

"I'll always be here for you, sis. Eat your food. We'll leave the subject alone for now, but we have five months to go before the baby gets here. That's our baby and it's going to be taken care of regardless."

We all finished eating and exited the restaurant and went to our cars. I pulled out first and led the way to the spa. When we arrived, Stone had set us up with the massage treatment, pedicures and manicures. Two hours later, I felt like a new woman. Celeste even looked better than she did before we entered the building.

"What are y'all about to do?" Sam asked when we stepped outside.

"I'm going to take a nap. Maria's hands got my ass sleepy as hell after the way she got the kinks out of my shoulders," I said laughing.

"I guess I'll go home and have a talk with Joe," Celeste said sadly.

"Fix your face. It's either the nigga is going to be happy, or he's not. Either way, come to my house if you need to. Call me if shit goes wrong, and I mean that," Sam said, giving her sister a hug.

"I'll call and check on you later," I said yawning. "Keep a positive mindset, everything will be okay."

I gave each of them a hug before I made my way to my car. As I sat in the driver's seat, my second phone rang. Getting it out of the armrest, Kenzie's name appeared on the screen. I thought about not answering, but I wanted to see what she had to say since it's been months since I'd talked to her.

"Hello."

"She's alive! What's been up with you, stranger?" she asked.

"Living."

"Why are you so dry with me? I think we need to talk about whatever is on your mind. You've distanced yourself for damn near a year, tell me, what's up?" Kenzie stated.

"You know, life. Ain't shit major," I said drily.

"Nah, I'm not buying that. Did I do something to you? Let that shit out. I consider you a sister and you just stopped fucking with me for no reason. There's something behind it and I want to know what it is."

"I have a life, Kenzie, and obviously it doesn't revolve around you," I snapped.

"Hold up, where's all the hostility coming from? Get that shit off your chest. There's something you're angry about and we can't get past the shit, if I don't know what the problem is."

"Ain't no hostility. Our friendship just ran its course. Ain't shit to talk about," I said truthfully.

"After everything we've been through, you couldn't tell me how the fuck you felt? You just decided to disappear like that would solve how you felt? We've been like family for years and this is the way you want to handle this shit?"

"It is what it is. You haven't considered me in a while, so—"

"What does that mean? If I didn't consider you, explain why I've been trying to contact yo' ass for months without a reply. I've been the one hounding you without getting anything in return. This is how I know that the problem lies within you, not me. If I had a fuckin' problem, I would've brought that shit to you and we would've gotten to the root of the problem a long time ago. Again, what's your problem with me, Nicassy?"

See, this is why I took on the job to get away from this bitch. Kenzie always thought she knew every muthafuckin' thing. I didn't have time for her power trip that day. There was no mistake on my part, and she was right, I had a problem with her ass.

"Kenzie, you think you're better than everybody."

"Nah, correction, that's your perception of me. Continue," she cut in.

Taking a deep breath, "It doesn't even matter," I said, not even wanting to voice my thoughts. It would be a waste of time anyway.

"So, you just gon' leave this shit in the air without talking it out? Keep dancing around the real reason you got your ass on your shoulders? Bet. Remember, I tried to talk this shit out, but you refused. I'm dropping this shit. It is what it is like you said. If you reach out, fine. If you don't, that's fine too. The ball is in your court. You, of all people, know kissing ass is not my forte."

Kenzie hung up in my face and I didn't feel an ounce of remorse behind it. Fuck her and her fucked-up attitude. Throwing the phone back in the armrest, I pulled out of the parking spot and peeled down the street, so I could beat traffic and make it to my bed.

Chapter 10

MaKenzie

Last night was the most fun I'd had in a very long time. Being back down south was where I needed to be. Chicago was a wonderful place, but Atlanta was home. Phantom was someone I could see myself having a lot of fun with. We were dancing and he was talking about all the ratchet females in the section on thirsty shit. The glares my sister and I were getting from some of them was ridiculous and funny as hell.

When me and Kayla went to the restroom and came back, all hell had broken loose because Loco was on straight bullshit. Monty rocked his ass because he was once again disrespecting, with his hatin' ass. I thought he learned earlier not to speak on my name, but I guess not. After that shit, I didn't want to party anymore.

My plans were to go home and relax, but I pulled up and Heat was sitting in wait like a stalker. I still couldn't believe he came out the side of his neck, telling me to stay away from Phantom. That shit was hilarious. How the fuck can a nigga tell you he needed space and expect you to sit back and wait? Not with me. Heat had the game fucked up and he was going to see what was passed up when he gave me the green light.

Getting to know Phantom was exactly what I planned to do. I didn't give a damn how many times Heat threatened me. I was the hardest female he would ever know. Breaking me down and cutting off my money flow, would never happen. I'm far from a weak bitch. Heat should know that shit didn't move me at all. Grind was my middle name and I knew how to go out and get the schmoney on my own.

My phone rang and I didn't feel like talking to anyone but ignoring phone calls was one thing I didn't do. I reached over on the other side of my bed and grabbed my phone to see who was disturbing my peace. Seeing my brother's name put a smile on my face and I quickly connected the call.

"Hey, bro! How's things going?"

"Kenzie, everything is good. I'm just chillin', but do we have a problem with one of those niggas down there?" Scony asked seriously.

"You talking about Loco, huh? Nah, that pussy ain't shakin' shit this way. He just hasn't processed that my balls are bigger than his yet. Monty took the opportunity to lay him on his ass for the bullshit he spit out his mouth. We good, I promise."

"It ain't shit for me to come down there and make that muthafucka disappear. You know that, right?"

"I already know. But this is my situation. You not about to come down here trying to take the shine from me. You had your turn, it's me and Kayla's turn now. If I need your help, I know how to hit your line."

Scony was quiet for a spell and I knew he was about to go deeper into some shit. Being who he was, the respect was high on the pedestal for him and I was ready to hear him out before responding. My brother cleared his throat and I took a sip of the lukewarm water I had on the nightstand.

"What is your take on what's going on with Kayla and Conte?"

"To be honest, brah. That's not my business. What I *will* say is this, Conte was wrong for reaching out to everyone but Kayla. Truthfully speaking, he is digging a deeper hole for himself because all he had to do was call and talk to her. Instead, he's making himself look like a weak nigga and you already know how Kayla is going to react to that. Ya boy fucked up whatever he thought he was going to accomplish by doing what he did."

"Sis, he didn't have anyone else to go to," Scony had the nerve to say.

"He could've talked to his *woman*! What would you do if Jade went to her girls about something the two of you were going through and that's how you heard about it? That shit wouldn't sit well with you, would it? Hell, nawl! Stop trying to justify what the fuck he did, brah." I paused to calm my nerves because I felt myself getting riled up.

"I haven't talked to Kayla about it one-on-one, I just heard what she said to Monty. It's a done deal for his ass and there's no coming back from what he has done. At least, that's how I'd be if it was me."

"Kenzie, you don't have a love bone in your body," he laughed. "I don't think any nigga out there has a chance to turn you into a lovin' woman. One day, I hope you would open your mind to love wholeheartedly."

"That would never happen. These niggas don't know how to appreciate a bitch that's willing to love them and give their all. Especially not a strong woman that's grinding, independent, and can hold her own. They flock to these needy bitches and I will never be one of them, ever in life. I'll move around and find someone that's cool with connecting pelvises before I utter the words, I love you to anybody. Y'all can have that shit. I'll leave my heart buried for as long as it needs to be."

"You will get past that eventually. Somebody is going to win you over. you just have to allow them in to love you."

"I'm not interested. I'm cool over here. Let's go back to Kayla and her fucked-up situation with Conte's soft ass. Stay out of that and let them deal with it on their own. I'm here to tell you, Scony, he fucked up."

"I'll tell him to hit her up—"

"Why the hell would you have to instruct him to call her? That's automatic, nigga. Get off my phone. Don't call me, I'll call you. Oh, call Nicassy because her jealousy is going to get her fucked up."

"What's going on?" Scony asked.

"I called her to see how she'd been and she popped off talking about I haven't been worried about her. Hell, I'd been calling her ass for months without being able to reach her. She came at me like I killed her dog or some shit. I ended the call and threw my hands up about the situation. She will need me before I need her. The sad part about it, I'm going to be right there regardless."

"Damn, that doesn't sound like her at all. I'll hit her up to make sure she's okay. Y'all being at odds isn't good for the business y'all have together. Smooth that shit out, Kenzie."

"I tried! She kept talking about life is the reason she's been distant, and her life didn't revolve around me. Where that shit came from, I'm still trying to figure it out," I said, getting out of the bed. I made my way to the bathroom and turned on the faucet. "You find out what her problem is. I have to get myself together so I can fill my empty stomach. I love you, bro."

"I love you too, Kenzie. Be careful out there."

"Always."

We ended the call and I jumped in the shower and brushed my teeth when I got out. I threw on a pair of leggings and a t-shirt, before making my way downstairs to make some breakfast. I had a taste for buttermilk pancakes, turkey bacon, cheese eggs, and hash browns. The alcohol and Za I smoked at the club had a bitch ready to eat everything in the house.

Putting all the ingredients on the counter, I raced back upstairs and rolled a wood, so I could get even hungrier. Grabbing my phone, I went back downstairs and went out in the backyard. One thing I didn't do was smoke in my home. I had a place where I could relax, in a gazebo fit for a diva.

I sat in my place of peace and mellowed out. My phone chimed and a text from an unrecognizable number came through. Opening the text, I read what it said.

(404) 555-0117: Hello, Storm. This is Phantom. I know it's early, but I wanted to take you out for breakfast. There's something I want to talk to you about. Where do you want to meet?

Reading the message over a couple times, I really didn't feel like leaving the house at that time. I smoked half of the wood before I even thought about responding. Phantom and I were introduced the day before and the thought of what he could possibly have to talk to me about was weighing heavy on my mind. Holding the wood tightly between my lips, I replied to Phantom's message.

Me: Hey Phantom. I wasn't planning to go anywhere this early. I'm about to cook breakfast. How about you slide over to my crib, we can eat here and talk. Address is 9008 Hickory Hills Court, see you when you get here.

Phantom didn't respond, so I continued to marvel in my peace. Turning on the music on my phone, I found the type of music I wanted to mellow out to. Sade's voice swooned through the speaker and her sultry voice calmed my soul. "Kiss of Life" was one of my favorite songs by her.

There must have been an angel by my side
Something heavenly led me to you
Look at the sky
It's the color of love

I had an old soul, thanks to my grandmother, and I would forever hold on to that feeling. I remember the Saturdays when she would have Kayla and I cleaning the house to old school music. Sade was one of her favorite artists and I grew to love her as well. I didn't start listening until after she was no longer a part of my life. That was my way of keeping her near and it actually worked.

I listened to a total of four songs before my phone chimed again. It was Phantom. I raised up from the bench while reading what he had to say.

(404) 555-0117: Where are you? I've been ringing the bell for the past five minutes. Did you give me the wrong address?

Chuckling all the way to the front of the house, I unlocked the door and pulled it open. Phantom was standing there with a scowl on his face, wearing a pair of basketball shorts, a black tee, and Nike slides with socks. He didn't put any thought into what he looked like early that morning. Phantom's appearance had me cringing on the inside.

"You didn't want a nigga in ya crib or something?"

"I was out back chillin' in the gazebo," I laughed. "I didn't even know you were here until you texted talking crazy. Get in here."

Phantom stepped inside while giving my body a onceover as he licked his lips. He sniffed a couple times as I turned away from the door after locking it. Folding his arms over his chest, he stared in my eyes with one of his eyebrows raised.

"I don't smell shit cooking, Storm. Where's the breakfast you lied about preparing?"

"It wasn't a lie. I went out back to smoke, but since I knew you were coming, I decided to wait until you arrived," I said, walking toward the bathroom. "Follow me so you can wash your hands, because you can't help me in the kitchen if you don't."

"Help you in the kitchen? I didn't come over here to be Chef Boyardee. What type of nigga you take me for? We could've gone out to eat by now."

"Phantom, breakfast is the easiest meal anyone could make. Plus, did you look in the mirror before you left the house? You're not going anywhere with me looking like a throwaway jack boy."

I laughed all the way to the bathroom, leaving his ass standing in the middle of the foyer. As I washed my hands, I looked up and Phantom was leaning on the door frame admiring my butt. We are going to be fuckin' soon if he doesn't stop undressing me with his eyes. I had to make sure he understood all I wanted was dick though.

"Wash your hands and meet me in the kitchen, perv," I said, walking past him.

"You haven't seen a perv in me, Storm. Also, you have seen me at my not-so best and a nigga was fly. So, a jack boy I've never been and never will be," he said causing me to glance over my shoulder at him. Working my ass off is something I've always done. I didn't start slinging dope, so don't put me in that category. We can go down memory lane when I come out of here, unless you want to come in and watch me drain the willy," he smirked.

"You got the wrong female, Phantom. Trying to sweet talk me will have you all in your feelings when I accept what you're offering and leave your ass high and dry. Don't forget to wash your hands."

I walked away and never looked back after the comment I made. Grabbing mixing bowls from the cabinet, I plugged in the tabletop griddle so it could get hot. As I added pancake mix in the bowl along with a little bit of milk, I stirred slowly, getting all the lumps out of the batter. When I had the batter just right, I tested the griddle to see if it was hot before placing a few strips of bacon on top of it.

"Is that turkey bacon?" Phantom said from the doorway.

"Yes, why? You don't eat turkey bacon?"

"I do. I don't eat pork, so I was making sure," he said, making his way deeper into the kitchen. "I'll pop these hash browns in the oven while you're taking care of that."

We were quiet as the two of us tried our best not to touch one another as we moved around the kitchen. Phantom started opening cabinet doors one by one until he found the one with the bowls in it. He broke a couple eggs in a bowl and opened the refrigerator as if he lived in my damn house. Phantom made it seem like he didn't know his way around the kitchen, but he was on real bullshit.

Watching him dice up spinach, mushrooms, onions, and red and green peppers, I was impressed. "Do you have olive oil? I'm going to need a skillet too," he said, without looking up.

Gathering everything he needed, I turned the bacon so it could cook a few more minutes before I removed it. Phantom added the oil and veggies to the skillet until they were tender enough to remove. He then added the spinach and cooked until it was kind of wilted. Removing the spinach from the pan, he added salt and pepper to the egg mixture and poured it into the skillet.

"You look like you know what you're doing," I said, pouring the pancake mixture on the griddle.

"I know a little bit. My mother made sure I could move around the kitchen with the best of 'em. I'll never go hungry because a female can't cook. If anything, she will be fending for herself fuckin' around with me," he laughed. "Nah, I take care of my women."

He added the veggies to one half of the omelet, along with shredded cheese and folded the egg mixture over. I handed him a plate and he slid the omelet onto it before he started the process again. I was flipping the pancakes and it seemed as if we would be finished about the same time. The timing was perfect as I poured two cups of orange juice after plating the pancakes and bacon.

Phantom turned off the stove as he took the hash browns out and placed two on each plate. He grabbed both of the dishes and I took the liberty of grabbing the glasses. When I sat across from him, he shocked me by saying a prayer. We ate in silence for a few minutes before Phantom wiped his mouth with a napkin and took a sip of his juice.

"This omelet is delicious! Thank you for helping me cook because you would've gotten some regular ass eggs out of me," I said after swallowing the food that was in my mouth.

"You're welcome. Maybe one day I'll come back to teach you how to make omelets. It's pretty easy though," he said, biting into a piece of bacon. "Tell me more about Storm."

"Nah, you first. I want to hear more about the guy that has never been a jack boy." Phantom ate silently for a spell then lowered his fork.

"I grew up here in Atlanta with my mother and my older brother, Fabian." The way he went completely silent told me something had hurt him in the past. "We made do with what we had and never complained about not having what everyone else had. What I mean is, we didn't have the latest fashions as our friends, but we made what we had look damn good."

"I understand that to a degree. Not for myself, but some of my friends endured that every day," I said, trying to fill the void of silence.

"My mama worked hard as hell to keep a roof over our head and food in our mouths. We had a nice house, but her paycheck went towards bills and after they were paid, we were able to get a shirt or a pair of pants here and there. Fabian wasn't satisfied with my mama working so hard and still barely being able to take care of the two of us. He started working at the post office after he graduated high school, because he didn't want to disappoint my mama by selling drugs."

Eating my food slowly, the pain in Phantom's eyes stood out. The vein in his temple twitched as his jaw clenched tightly. He pushed his plate away and folded his hands in front of him on the table.

"The year I graduated high school my life changed drastically. Fabian was shot and killed in a drive-by shooting coming home from work. He wasn't the target, but the non-shooting muthafuckas should've aimed correctly. I made a vow that I would find out who took my brother away from me, and I did. It was the first time I did a hit without anyone seeing me do it."

"I'm so sorry for your loss," I said sympathetically.

"You don't have to be sorry. It's been damn near ten years, and even though it hurts every time I speak about my brother, I know I got justice for him. It's my job to get justice for anyone that has wronged someone's family. That's why I decided my occupation today."

Hearing Phantom tell the story of his brother brought out emotions I never felt in all the years of me being in the business. He had a different reason for doing what he does than I did. The reason I do it is simple. I like getting scum off the streets. I don't care who they are, what nationality they are, or their gender. It may sound cruel, but to me, it really isn't.

"What's your story, Storm?" Phantom asked, starting to eat again.

"My story is nothing compared to yours. I was taught how to use a weapon at an early age, and I was granted the opportunity to make money doing it. At first, it was about making my own money but in time, it turned into getting justice for others when they couldn't accomplish it on their own."

I looked through Phantom as I thought about all the back stories I'd heard, with each client that came to Heat for help. There were no questions asked as I read through the documents before I went out to complete a mission. The rush that flowed through me gave me the courage to go hard to end a life.

"I was raised by my grandmother after my mother passed away. I didn't *need* to do this for financial gain, my brother took care of our family with no problem. The reason I do this is because it's what I want to do. I'm anxious for Heat to give me my first assignment. I haven't been so ready in two years and the excitement is building.

Phantom stared at me with admiration. He shook his head and laughed. "I can tell right now, you're a beast. I see how you get down, shawty. Speaking of Heat, what's going on between the two of y'all?"

"Why would you ask me that?" I quizzed.

"He called me last night, saying you were off limits. When he said you belonged to him, I laughed and told him let the best man win."

I got pissed because Heat had no right to say anything to Phantom when it came to me. His ass was sitting at home, monitoring what the fuck was happening in the club, which was fine. But monitoring what I was doing and who I was doing it with, was a major problem.

"Wait a minute! He had the audacity to call you and say stay away from me? Heat has lost his ever lovin' mind with this shit. Let me tell you about me and Heat. There's nothing going on between the two of us. We had something going on but that's been over for years. I don't know how long you've worked for him, but it's evident he's fuckin' with Summer. That's where he'd better direct all his bullshit."

"Calm down. I just wanted to see what I was getting into, because the last thing I want is any friction within the team. I'm not about to go head-to-head with anybody over a female. It's not worth it to me."

"What is there to wonder about? I haven't given you any indication that anything would go on between us. Even if I did, Heat can't stop me from poppin' my pussy for nobody. His ass is grown and has a whole muthafuckin' woman! I'm not her." I was getting madder by the minute because Heat was acting like a little ass boy.

"You don't have to give me anything, I know what I'm trying to do, Storm. I'm gon' tread lightly and put the ball in your court. It will be solely up to you how this play out."

"While we're on the subject, I want to know you on another level too. The way my heart is set up, I don't need you getting too involved with me and fall in love. That's not what I want in my life right now. So, to lead you on is something I never intend to happen."

"Storm, you can't let something that happened in your past stifle what can possibly happen in your future. Love isn't for everybody, I understand that. But don't push your soulmate away. That person may not be me but leave the opportunity to open for whomever it may be."

"I'll lay it out on the table for you. I'm willing to spend time with you, and we can have sexual relations, but I'm telling you now, it's a friends with benefits type of deal. Nothing more."

"I'm not trying to just fuck, Storm. So, we can take this shit slow without any expectations. Whatever happens, there's no labels being put in place on my end. Enough about that, are you finished eating?"

Pushing my plate toward Phantom, I watched as he gathered all the dishes and stood to his feet. His ass was moving around my kitchen as if he lived there and it made me feel some type of way. I went into the living room to let my food digest by turning on the video console, loading *Call of Duty*. I placed my headphones on my head and connected to the internet so I could talk shit with the niggas online.

"What you know about *Call of Duty?*" Phantom asked, sitting next to me on the couch.

"Everything," I said, without taking my eyes off the TV. "Grab the other controller and the headset and choose a side. I can show you better than I can tell you."

"Man, you confident in everything you do. Let me get in on this shit. I'm getting on yo' side and you better protect a nigga."

We played the game and smoked for a while. Before I knew it, the sun had set and we were still talking big shit like best friends. It felt good to just enjoy the moment and I looked forward to sharing another day with Phantom.

Meesha

Chapter 11

Phantom

As I drove toward my home, Layla sat with her head against the window. My big baby was so sleepy and worn out. Pulling up to my home, I parked in the garage and hurried to get Layla into the house. She woke up soon as I placed her on top of the bed.

"Get undressed and get in bed, baby."

"Daddy, you know I'm not going to bed without taking a shower. You forgot what you taught me? You slippin', man!"

Layla climbed off the bed and went to her dresser and open the drawer. She pulled out her nightgown and headed out the room to the bathroom leaving me there with my mouth open. Yes, I taught my daughter about hygiene, because her mother didn't think it was important enough to hear from her. The job was put on my shoulders and I make it my business to teach my daughter how to be the princess she is destined to be. She will know she is going to be a queen.

The queen that took over my thoughts was no other than Storm. We had a wonderful time and she left a lot on my mind to think about. The two of us clicked after our initial conversation, and then the shit talking began as we went toe-to-toe with the tools on the video game. It didn't dawn on me until that moment, she knew my real name, but I failed to ask hers. There was still so much I didn't know about Storm, but time would bring more to light.

I wasn't looking forward to the meeting with Heat and the team the following day, because I had a feeling there would be tension on Heat's part. Nothing happened between Storm and I, but Boss-man wasn't green to the way I moved. It also didn't help that I had basically told him I was willing to do anything to get with Storm. The challenge was put out there and I wasn't going to take it back.

Shouldn't no nigga be jealous of another about a bitch, that's a muthafuckin' female trait. Heat was showing his bitch side and I was more than ready to punch his ass in the chest to force him to man the fuck up. Hopefully, it won't go that far but I was ready for whatever. He was too old to let shit like that cloud his judgement.

I stood from Layla's bed and she walked in dressed for the night. She put her dirty clothes in the hamper and crawled in the bed. Staring at my one and only child, I watched as she snuggled under the covers with her hand under her chin.

"Daddy, would you please stop looking at me? I'm trying to get my beauty rest," Layla said without opening her eyes.

"Beauty rest? You are already beautiful." Walking toward the bed, I crawled in as Layla opened her eyes.

"Don't you dare!" She laughed, snatching the pillow from under her head. "I'm not in the mood. I'm sleepy!"

I pulled the cover back and started tickling Layla on her stomach and under her neck. The squeals she let out was too cute and I loved hearing them. She squirmed around, trying to get away from me. Layla grabbed my hands and hopped out of the bed.

"You playing too much, Daddy! Get out of my room. I quit," she laughed.

"Okay, baby. I quit. I'll see you in the morning. I love you."

"I love you too, Daddy. I want blueberry pancakes for my pain and suffering."

"Pain and suffering? You were laughing, Layla."

"You could've made me pee on myself. That would've been devastating if it had happened," she smirked.

"Little con artist. Blueberry pancakes it is. Anything else?"

"Yeah, eggs and lots of bacon!"

"You got it," I said, kissing her forehead as she got comfortable in the bed for the second time.

Turning off the light and pulling up the door, I headed to my bedroom to get ready for my own shower. Twenty minutes later, I was in bed with the remote in hand when my phone started ringing. Getting up, I walked to the dresser and Tiff's name was displayed on the screen.

"What's up?" I said when I answered.

"I want you to know that Butch has to have therapy on his legs because you messed up his muscles. He has to learn to walk again."

"Tiff, do you think I give a fuck about that nigga? Yo' stupid ass is lucky I didn't kill him. Now he can live another day to whoop yo' ass again. Get the fuck off my phone with the bullshit."

"Bring my daughter home, Phantom. I miss her," Tiff said calmly.

"You need to clear yo' head for a couple weeks. Nurse yo' nigga back to health or something, but Layla is not coming back to that bullshit. The only way she can come back, is if that nigga is put out on his ass. It's all on you."

"I'll tell the police you were the one that shot Butch!"

"I know you will, that's why his ass only got two to the legs. There's no serious case for that shit. I'll be back on the streets in no time. Then both of you muthafuckas will come up missing. Try me," I said, bangin' on her stupid ass.

What I did to Tiffany's dude was going to have some repercussions, but I wasn't worried about that shit. I don't condone a nigga putting his hands on any woman. There were many occasions when I could've gone upside her head and didn't, on the strength of Layla alone. Tiffany better think long and hard about her next move, because I believed she would be in the midst of the bullshit with her dude. Pushing the conversation with Tiff to the back of my mind, I turned over in bed and closed my eyes.

***

I woke up later than expected the next day, but I had to cook for my baby girl. Adding eggs to our plates, I picked them up and placed them on the table as Layla entered the kitchen, looking like a replica of me in female form. Her hair was all over her head, but she was still beautiful in my eyes.

"Good morning, sleepyhead. How did you sleep?" I asked as she sat in the chair that she deemed hers.

"I slept good. Thank you for making me pancakes, Daddy. You always come through." Layla said a silent prayer and started eating her food immediately. "What's our plans for the day?"

"Well, I have some business to take care of, but that's not for a few hours. We can do whatever you like, but I'll be taking you to your grandma's afterward."

"That's sounds like a plan. It's better than going back to Mama's house," she said, with a mouthful of pancakes.

"Layla, what I tell you about talking with food in your mouth?"

"It's rude and not ladylike," she responded, holding her head down.

"Lift your head. There's nothing to be ashamed about. I will keep reminding and guiding you of what's right and wrong, baby. It's the only way you will learn from your mistakes."

"I understand, Daddy. In order to be a queen, I have to present myself in that manner. Always hold my head high and never let my crown fall."

Layla recited what I'd taught her with precision, and I was proud. It let me know she had been listening to everything I've ever said to her and sucked it up like a sponge. I smiled and sat at the table with my baby, nodding my head in agreeance.

"Daddy, I have one request before we leave this house," she said, taking a sip of her juice.

"What's that?'

"You have to do your black Dad magic and comb my hair! It's hideous."

I almost choked on my bacon, laughing. "I got you, baby. One ponytail coming up soon as we finish eating."

Thirty minutes later, Layla was dressed and sitting on the floor in the living room, while I brushed her hair. I'd learned to comb my daughter's hair when she was about two. Tiffany was always running the streets, so I had to do what needed to be done. Layla had to be fresh from head to toe before she exited the house.

I had forty-five minutes to get Layla to my moms and make it to the club on time. My mama was waiting on us to pull up, because I called her ahead of time to ask if Layla could come over. After getting cussed out for asking, she hung up on me. My mother was my savior because I knew I had help when it came to my daughter.

There weren't many I trusted because so much was going on with children these days.

Layla jumped out of my car soon as I stopped in my mother's driveway. I didn't get a kiss, hug, nothing. "Aye!" I called out as I exited my whip. "Where's my love?"

"I'm sorry, Daddy," Layla said, running towards me. She jumped in my arms and hugged my neck tightly before planting a kiss on my cheek. "I love you. Be safe."

"I will, baby. Be good, I love you too."

Watching my daughter skip back up the steps, I got in my ride and backed out of the driveway. Storm's beautiful face flashed before my eyes and I couldn't wait to see her. It took less time than usual to get to the club. I guess my anticipation got the best of me.

Spotting Storm's car, I hurried to get out of my car and headed inside. Getting closer to the door of the conference room, I could hear Storm's voice and it was like a bird singing a lullaby to my ears. She wasn't cursing, screaming, nor threatening to kill anybody. As I pushed the door open, Storm and Kane were sitting side-by-side and the smile on her face was intoxicating. When she turned toward the door, I saw a small twinkle in her eye, but maybe I was mistaken.

"What up, cuz?" Khaos said, nodding his head as he gave his attention back to Kane.

"You got it. Hey, everybody." I took a seat at the opposite end of the table and sat back in the chair observing things.

My cousin was smitten with her, just as I was with her sister. I took that moment to study the two sisters. Being able to tell them apart was something I needed to figure out expeditiously. Taking in both of their features, I couldn't see any difference between the two. By me staring extremely hard, I drew the attention of everyone in the room.

"Phantom, what's going on with you? Is there something about Storm and Kane you want to tell us about?" Khaos asked.

"I knew something was fishy about they ass!" Loco bellowed out.

"Don't start that shit, nigga. Ain't shit going on," I said before his ass could get started. "Where is the boss?"

Ignoring my question, Storm cut her eyes at Loco with a scowl on her face. I stood to my feet and walked over to her side and rubbed the small of her back. Her expression softened and Kane smirked as she glanced between the both of us.

"Let that shit go," I whispered. Storm turned her head and I shook mine to silence her.

"Yeah, keep her ass quiet before she gets hurt in this mutha-fucka," Loco continued to taunt Storm. "Somebody needs to explain her place in this business."

Loco was pushing his luck and the tension in Storm's back didn't go unnoticed. I knew if he kept going, there would be nothing I could do to stop whatever took place. Loco was sitting right next to Kane, but all eyes were on her sister.

"Bitches were meant to be home, barefoot and pregnant. Not trying to work with the big dogs in the streets."

Kane jumped up from her seat and all I saw was her hand going across Loco's head. Blood started spurting everywhere as she pistol-whipped him repeatedly. Khaos jumped up to avoid getting the blood splattered on his clothes, but it was a little too late for that. Kane was beating the fuck out of Loco and I didn't see it coming to a halt anytime soon.

"I'm tired of hearing yo' fuckin' mouth! Now you have to worry about the jokes that's going to come from me beating yo' dumb ass!"

Khaos grabbed Kane around the waist and carried her to the other side of the room. The white pantsuit she wore was covered in Loco's blood and her light brown eyes were coal black from where I stood. Kane was struggling to get out of Khaos' grip, to no avail. Dreux was checking on Loco and scrambled to get his phone out of his pocket.

"Aye, come to the club now! Bring your medical bag, I have an emergency," he said, disconnecting the call. At that moment, the door opened and Heat walked in, to total mayhem.

"What the fuck!" his voice boomed. Heat looked around the room but when his eyes landed in the direction of me and Storm, the fire in them could've set the entire room ablaze. Rocko handed Dreux a towel and addressed his boss.

"Man, we gotta do something about Loco. He can't keep disrespecting Storm and think she is going to just sit back and let the shit go on."

Heat walked over to exam the damage done to Loco and swung around to Storm. "I've told you about your attitude! Let that nigga talk. He will get tired at some point," Heat huffed.

"See, get your shit right and point the finger where it belongs. I didn't touch that nigga and he's lucky too. How many times would it take for him to come at you the way he seems to continuously come at me?" Storm asked.

"He would never come at me like that!"

"Exactly! He will give me the same muthafuckin' respect! I'm not waiting for one of y'all to stand up for me. I'm standing up for myself at all times. Stop acting like you don't know, Heat. Loco thought because I didn't move, he wouldn't get touched. There's another me by my side every minute of the day. I told you before to tell this nigga about me, you didn't listen and that's on you."

Storm got up and walked out of the room as Daniel, our personal physician, was coming in. Daniel went right to work on Loco while we all stood in silence. Kane was still struggling to get away from Khaos but instead of letting her go, he escorted her out of the room.

"I don't want to start every meeting with bullshit! Y'all gon' have to learn how to defuse the situations when you see them getting out of hand. We have to work together and get along as a team. From this moment on, there will be a fine with all involved parties that bring negativity into this establishment."

"Nah, you need to teach Loco some respect. The shit he says and does to the bitches outside, won't work with Storm and Kane. Until he realizes that, he gon' keep getting fucked up by the hands of two strong ass females," I said, standing up for the twins. "You can keep that fine shit to yo'self, I'm gon' address anything brought my way, even if it's within yo' establishment. You not about to try to Ike Turner me. I'm not payin' nobody's fare unless it's taxes."

Heat was mad as hell, but I didn't give a fuck. He was directing all of this towards me because his feelings were activated over Storm. That was between the two of them, it had zero to do with me. Hopefully, his female tendencies didn't interfere with business, because it would be fucked up for him to lose everything behind a woman who was done with his ass.

"I need a spot to lay him down, his head requires staples," Daniel announced.

"Put him on the couch. Everybody else, get out. I will contact y'all when I reschedule the meeting. This is the type of shit I'm talking about! Business is being pushed back for nonsense!" Heat was pissed, but he was directing his anger at the wrong muthafuckas. Loco was the one that needed a rude awakening.

"Heat, I'm speaking for everyone right now," Dreux said before he got to the door. "Loco gon' have to change his way of thinking or shit gon' get worse. I'm not about to be losing money behind his hot head ass. Holla at him because it's ridiculous."

Dreux slung the door open and stalked out. Loco was moaning in agony and I glanced over at him as everyone filed out of the conference room. The only thing I could do was shake my head. Watching a few seconds longer as Daniel administered the anesthesia, before working to close the gashes on Loco's head.

"Stay away from Storm, Phantom. I won't say it again," Heat said as I crossed the threshold.

"From what I heard, what y'all had ran its course. Get ya panties out ya ass, Heat. Hit my line when you're ready to talk business. Until then, don't' come to me with no more bullshit about Storm."

Leaving his ass standing there, I made my way to the front of the club. Everyone was outside congregating in the parking lot. As I walked up, they turned their attention to me. Storm was pulling on a wood as she paced back and forth. Kane was leaning on the side of Khaos' car. She had changed into a pair of jeans, a t-shirt and a fresh pair of Nikes.

"Man, Phantom, what the fuck is wrong with Heat? He acts like Storm is the cause of all of this. Why is he coming at her like this?" Rocko asked.

"I'll tell you why," Storm said, walking over. "He is mixing his personal life with business. Not a good combination at all. I'll let it be known, I used to fuck with Heat—"

"Storm, you don't have to air what you do," Dreux said, cutting her off. "That's between you and Heat."

"Dreux, if you can honestly say he didn't let on that he's in his feelings back there, I'll shut up." Storm waited for Dreux to respond. When he didn't, she continued her point. "Exactly! He walked in and saw Phantom close to me and he became belligerent and aimed his anger towards me! I'll bet every dime in my pocket Heat had something to say to Phantom before he left that room."

"I doubt he did, because Heat ain't built like that," Big Will chimed in.

"Well, that nigga ain't Ford tough. He did tell me to stay away from Storm. Heat is my boss, he's not my father. Nobody can tell me what to do with my life. That shit is between them. I want to know what the fuck we gon' do about Loco. He's been moving real shaky and it didn't start Friday. Something is going on with him, and I think we need to keep an eye out for that shit."

"I agree, fam. Loco is using the twins as a way to get shit off his chest. If he knew what was good for him, he'd pipe that shit down and stop coming for them," Rocko laughed. "Kane beat his ass like Caine did Chauncey in *Menace to Society*."

That shit was true and I pictured that shit as I laughed hard as fuck. Khaos handed me the spiff as I coughed from choking myself. Kane didn't find the joke funny at all. She was standing with a mug on her stoned face. Once I stopped laughing and inhaled the herb, I tried my hand at softening her up.

"Kane, don't let Loco get to you. You and Storm both have gave him a taste of what y'all about. Hopefully, he takes heed to that shit and back the fuck up. Next time, he will have to answer to one of us because he is trying to manhandle women and failed miserably, twice."

"I blame Heat, because he should've been on his ass about what he had done on Friday," Storm said, sitting on top of Khaos' hood.

"Man, if you don't get yo' ass off my car! Put a dent in it, you paying for it!"

Storm laughed and didn't move an inch. One thing my cousin didn't play about was his whips. That's part of the reason he didn't have any kids, he spent all his damn money on the upkeep of his vehicles.

"Man, shut all that up," Storm said, waving her hand at Khaos. "Look, we should go out and have some fun. Heat will be calling with assignments any day. We have at least until Tuesday to live it up. As a matter of fact, it's Memorial Day weekend, somebody should host a barbeque."

"I'm down for that. Phantom, we should do it at yo' crib."

How the fuck my house become the designated barbeque spot? I didn't want these fools in my shit. Hell nawl, that was a negative for me. In fact, Loco would get murked bringing his bullshit to my crib.

"Nope, nope, nope, nope. Why you volunteering my crib? You the one with the high-class barbeque pit and the swimming pool, cuz. In fact, you just had the surround sound outside yo' yard. Seems to me, yo' shit would be a better option. Plus, Loco isn't invited to none of my shindigs no mo'."

"Shidddd, that nigga ain't invited to my shit either, fuck you thought? It's all good, we can have it at my crib. What y'all bringing, because I'm not footing the bill for all you muthafuckas. I got whateva Kane want, though," Khaos said, winking at her.

"You good, I can handle it," Kane shot back.

The twins were so damn independent, it wasn't funny. When I hear females say they don't need a nigga for shit, most of the time they frontin', but Kane and Storm are of another caliber and don't need shit they can't get themselves. I had to figure out a way to get in Storm's heart, because my pockets don't stand a chance.

Chapter 12

Heat

After Daniel finished with Loco, Big Will helped me get him in my whip, after telling me about the conversation Storm aired out in the parking lot. The shit was nothing to me because I stood on what the fuck I said about the matter. Phantom will not have what I deemed as mine and that was it.

Parking in front of his crib, I got out and walked around to help him out. Loco had awakened as I turned down his block, but he had yet to say anything. Kane did a number on his ass and I felt the pain for him. He looked like that damn Chucky doll by the face and the shit was somewhat spooky.

Mya, Loco's baby mama, opened the door and walked on the porch as I helped him around his waist leading the way up the driveway. I controlled the pace of how fast he walked, making sure he didn't fall. Loco raised his head and I heard Mya gasp as she raced down the steps.

"Oh my God, what happened to you, baby?" she shrieked.

"He got—"

"Some niggas jumped me outside the club as I got out my car. I'll be straight," he said, cutting me off as he made his way up the stairs one at a time.

I wasn't about to correct him on his story, because I wouldn't want my woman to know I got my ass beat by a bitch either. That shit was embarrassing for the whole team to witness, let alone his woman finding out about it. Mya was one of those females that would hold on to the bad shit Loco did and hold it over his head for eternity. She always looked for his downfalls and he kept placing the ammo in her hands to fire off.

"What the fuck did you do now? It was your mouth, wasn't it? Loco, you gon' have to learn how to just ignore certain shit or learn how to fight. I'm tired of nursing yo' ass back to health over stupid shit."

"Take yo' ass somewhere, Mya! I know how to fight. Them niggas be sneakin' me and you know it. Go check on my son," Loco said, flopping down on the couch.

Mya walked out of the room, mad as hell, mumbling under her breath as she went to check on Leonardo Jr. I sat on the loveseat across from Loco and stared at him intensely. When he was finally lying comfortably on the couch, I took a deep breath before I addressed him.

"Loco, let me tell you something. Storm and Kane ain't going anywhere. They have been on the team for almost four years and have proved they belong. It's either you gon' accept that, or you will continue to bump heads with them. Your choice."

"Man, look, I'm not about to give two bitches the same respect I give the niggas on the team. We don't need them!"

"That's where you're wrong. Both of them are thorough and I stand by them in any and everything they do. Hell, I even stand by them for standing up to yo' ass. That showed me they still got what the fuck they left with two years ago."

"And what's that?" Loco asked, turning his head in my direction.

"Heart, nigga! They ain't all bark with no bite. As you saw firsthand, they can back shit up without hesitation. That's how the fuck I need you to be at all times. Leave them the fuck alone, Loco. You won't win against them, trust me."

I stood to leave and Loco just closed his eyes without responding. It was his way of not addressing the real issue, but if he knew like I did, Loco would wise up and let the animosity go. Mya walked down the hall with LJ in her arms. Waving goodbye, I stormed out the door and jumped in my whip.

Pushing the gas pedal past eighty, I hurried to get home so I could get to work and find some jobs for the team. I was glad for the disruption between the twins and Loco, because I would've had to explain why I didn't have any work for them when I entered. Stone had cut a nigga all the way off, but I had access to all his clients. A nigga like me was going to utilize that shit to my advantage once Stone was out of the picture.

Noticing Summer's car parked in my driveway as I pulled up, I shook my head because I didn't feel like dealing with her. Summer had been on my ass ever since she found out Storm was back in town. She was focusing on the wrong shit, instead of the position she had in my life. What I wasn't going to do was go back and forth with her every time I was in her presence. Parking on the side of her midnight black Durango, I eased out of the driver's seat and made my way up to the house.

Summer was sitting at the kitchen table with a bottle of Hennessy in front of her. Right off the bat, I knew she was full of alcohol and there was going to be a confrontation. As I got closer to where she was sitting glaring at the wall, Summer turned swiftly in my direction.

"Why are you indulging in that bottle in the middle of the day, Summer?" I asked, taking a seat on the opposite side of the table.

Lifting the glass to her lips, Summer took a huge gulp of the dark liquid and winced as it traveled down her throat. She slammed the glass down on the table and peered at me angrily, while sitting back with an attitude. The bullshit was about to begin. Once she got the shit off her chest, I was going to end the so-called relationship I had with her. Putting up with the back and forth shit over nothing was one thing I wasn't about to do.

"You were with her, wasn't you, Heat?"

"Summer, who the fuck you talking about?" I asked.

"MaKenzie! You know exactly who I'm talking about," she screamed. "I was there when you were worried about who the fuck she's getting close to. Why does it matter if she's trying to get to know Phantom, if you're with me?"

True enough, I'd been fucking with Summer since Kenzie left to go back to Chicago, but I never made her my woman. Sleeping with her and giving her a little bit of time does not equate to her being my woman. This is the reason I stay to myself without agreeing to a relationship. Females know what they are getting into, then want to make it into something it's not.

"Summer, what the hell are you talking about? You in this muthafucka drinking and in your feelings about the one thing we agreed on. You are not my woman! Don't question me about shit I do. While you're worried about Kenzie, you should be worrying about yourself. I'm a single man and yes, I fuck you whenever I feel like it, and that's it. We don't have a title for what we're doing, and I would like to keep it that way."

"I have keys to your fuckin' home! Why is that if I'm not shit to you, Heat?"

"Give them muthafuckas to me. This is a subject we will never have to address again," I said, holding my hand out. "You're right, I had you thinking there was more going on, but I've told you from the jump not to take this shit serious. I'm not ready to settle down, Summer. Far as Kenzie is concerned, mind ya business," I said, standing to my feet.

"I'm not giving you nothing! There was a reason you gave me the spare key. I should be able to ask simple questions without you getting upset when I present the obvious. You don't give a fuck about me, so why are you with me?"

Staring at the woman sitting at my kitchen table, I kind of felt bad she didn't get the picture. What we had was pure sexual, and she let her feelings get the best of her and now she was all in her emotions. I played a major part in how she felt, but I didn't lead her on in any type of way. What we have is just that, nothing outside of sex.

"Summer, you don't have to unass the keys, but just know, you won't be able to enter my shit at your leisure after today. Stop thinking so hard and enjoy the moment. We good as long as you know your place. That doesn't mean I don't have feelings for you. We are just not in a committed relationship."

"You still haven't answered my question. Why are you worried about who the bitch is dealing with?"

"If you stop worrying about her, your days would be brighter. Are you trying to chill with me, or do you want to continue arguing? If it's the latter, you can take your ass in the guest room and go to sleep until you sober up. I have enough shit on my plate and don't need to add more to it."

Leaving Summer's ass in the kitchen, I headed upstairs to my bedroom as my phone started ringing. Tornado's name displayed on the screen and that added to my frustrations. Swiping the button on my phone, I place it to my ear, closing my bedroom door.

"Yo' ass better be just getting out of jail or something," my voice boomed through the phone.

"Nah, I'm trying to catch Stone in the act with the young girls you said he be messing with. There's no proof of that, Heat. He's never around any underaged girls. Why am I really here?"

"I know muthafuckin' well you ain't questioning me, bitch! I sent yo' ass down there to kill that muthafucka! All you needed to do was put a bullet in his muthafuckin' head. I know what it is, you done got friendly with the nigga and now you got questions. Bad move, Tornado."

"It was a bad move on your part! Don't scream at me about the faulty shit you're on. We kill people that has done malicious shit to others. Like, the molester you made this man out to be would've been the perfect candidate, if the shit was true. I see right now this is a personal vendetta of yours, Heat. Don't bring me in your bullshit. I'm aborting the mission and fuck you and your business! I quit!"

"You aren't allowed to—" I looked down at the phone and the bitch had hung up on my ass. Calling Tornado's phone back, it went straight to voicemail and the shit pissed me off. I tried being nice to these bitches, but they were going to keep trying me.

The fact that Stone was still breathing pissed me off to the highest level of pisstivity. I sent Tornado's muthafuckin' ass to Houston nine months ago and the bitch done fell in love. Hearing how she was questioning me let me know what it was.

Stone was my connect for all the jobs I received for the team. Shit had been going downhill because the nigga called one day, asking about the distribution of the money to my team. That was none of his fuckin' business. All he had to concentrate on was the jobs getting done. Anything else wasn't his concern and that's where he violated with me.

I sent in Tornado so she could eliminate his ass and it hadn't been done yet. It's all good. I was giving her ass two weeks to get it together, before I throw a monkey wrench in her shit. One thing a muthafucka wasn't going to do was try to play me like a scrub. Storm was already pressing her luck with Phantom.

Stevie Wonder could see the two slicksters trying to act as if they didn't have a connection. I peeped that shit when I walked into the conference room and Phantom was standing there, rubbing Storm's back to calm her down. Something was brewing with Kane and Khaos as well, but that wasn't my business. Storm was mine and I'd told her hardheaded ass to stay the fuck away from the nigga.

First, Storm wanted to come back with a new attitude and dismiss everything I told her not to do, Kane is walking around beating niggas like they stole something, now Tornado wants to come at me like she's the boss. I'm going to show them how I kill Savage Storms, and Tornado is about to be used as an example.

Chapter 13

Khaos

We ended up going to get everything for the barbeque before we hit the streets for the night. We went bowling and I lost so much money to Storm and Kane, I wanted to shoot their asses and get my shit back. They hustled all of us the first game, because they played the part of not knowing how to play the sport. As we started the second game and put a wager on it, they turned into professionals and ripped us off.

It was six in the morning and I was up cleaning meat before I seasoned it. The ribs were marinated when I got home and I was glad I decided to work, because I couldn't sleep thinking of ways to get my money back. Placing the wings in a pan, I panned the Italian sausages and put them to the side. Arranging the shish kabobs using steak, red, yellow, and green peppers. Adding zucchini and mushrooms to finish them off, I decided at the last minute to make some with chicken breast to give a variety to choose from. The hotdogs and burgers would be last to go on the grill.

Storm and Kane was supposed to come over early to help cook the sides, but I may start them on my own since I was in the mood. One thing my mama taught me to do was cook. Walking outside to the backyard, I fired the grill up and let the charcoal smolder. There was a lot of food and I didn't plan on cooking when everyone arrived, because I wanted to have a good time too, shit.

I had been working for about five hours when the doorbell sounded. Glancing at the television to see who was at my crib without calling first, a smile spread across my face when I saw Storm and Kane standing on the porch. I grabbed a paper towel and made my way to the foyer to let them in. Opening the door, I stood looking stupid because I didn't know which one of the twins I was crushing on. What I didn't want to do was flirt with the wrong twin.

"Are you going to let us in, or are we cooking right here on the porch?"

"Oh, my bad. Come in, ladies," I said, stepping to the side, making sure to avoid using names. "Welcome to my home."

"This is nice, Khaos. I know you didn't decorate yourself. This has a woman's touch to it."

"You are correct, Storm, it does. My mother is an interior decorator and she got ya boy right." I beamed as I watched them walk slowly through my house, but that was short-lived because I fucked up.

"Nope, wrong twin," Kane laughed. "That's one of the reasons I know you're not ready to start anything with me. You would have to be able to decipher who I am, when me and my sister are together."

"That shit is impossible, shawty. Y'all are identical as fuck! There's no way to know one from the other."

"Not true at all. It just takes a while for one to figure us out," Storm said.

As I led them to the kitchen, I locked Kane's image in my mind so I would know who she was for the rest of the day. Both of them wore jean shorts with tank tops. The difference was, Storm's shirt was a light green color and Kane's was purple, but both had "Sassy, Moody, Nasty" on the front.

Both of them were like giddy kids when they stepped into my huge kitchen. They wasted no time washing their hands. I just hoped they knew how to throw down and the food was edible enough to eat. Giving both of them aprons to protect their clothes, I showed them where everything was so they could start making the coleslaw, cold spaghetti, potato salad, macaroni and cheese, and baked beans.

As Kane glanced around, she spotted a bunch of bananas and got excited. "Can I use some of those to make a banana pudding for dessert?" she asked.

"Hell yeah, I love banana pudding," I said happily. "I actually bought everything you will need, because I was going to ask my mama to make me one. I know how, but I like hers better. Maybe you can push her out the way, and hook a nigga up if it's good," I smirked.

"I can and won't ever try to take the place of your mama. Cherish everything about her while you can, because it can be snatched away in a heartbeat."

Her statement made me admire her more because regardless how hard she appeared to be, she had a soft side and I wanted to see what's to it. Nodding my head, I went outside to check on the kabobs I had on the grill, leaving them to burn in the kitchen. My phone rang as I stepped out the door and I retrieved it out of my pocket.

"What up, fam?"

"Yo! Get ready to let a nigga in, I'm down the street," Phantom yelled.

"Why are you screaming? I hope you stopped at the liquor store, since you collected money and shit, nigga. The gate to the yard is open, come through the back."

"Damn, I forgot I was supposed to get the drinks. Fuck man, why didn't you send a text to remind me?"

I just hung up on his ass because he always needed somebody to remind him about something. I had much love for my cousin, but he made my ass itch sometimes. Phantom and I had been tight since we were youngins. We were the same age, six months apart and people always thought we were brothers instead of cousins. Our mothers were pregnant together and in turn, we did everything together as kids and as adults too.

"Uncle K!" Layla screeched as Phantom held the gate open for her. She ran into my arms before I could wipe my hands good.

"Hey, big girl," I said, swooping her up into the air. "How you been?"

"Good. I've been keeping Grandma Karla company, but daddy said he was coming to see you and we wanted to come to."

"We? Who else is here?" I asked, shooting my cousin a quizzing look. I noticed Phantom was holding a box of alcohol and wanted to knock his head off his shoulders for lying. My aunt Karla entered the yard and I rushed over and kissed her cheek, while using my free arm to hug her tightly.

Auntie Karla smirked at me and I shook my head. She knew I didn't like anyone other than her and my mama cooking in my kitchen. It's been a minute since I'd had any woman in my space, and I guess that was my aunt's way of telling me it was time. In a way, I kind of agreed with her.

"Kannon, I'm gonna let you check on that meat you burning over there, and make sure Kayla isn't burning down your house. Put Layla's big ass down too. That's the reason she's so damn spoiled now. If it's not her daddy, it's you always catering to her. Come here, girl," she said as I put Layla down for the second time. "I was talking to you too, missy."

Kenzie laughed, but she moved her feet to head into the house. When the women left us alone, I checked the meat and removed the kabobs off the grill. The smell of them were delectable and made my mouth water.

"Man, how long you been cooking, nigga?" Phantom asked, walking to the table and started taking the bottles out the box.

"Shit, since about seven or eight, but I've been up since six. I wanted to make sure everything was done before folks got here. All the meat is warming in the oven. The ladies are whipping up the sides and we'll be good after I cook the hamburgers, hotdogs, and the Italian sausages. After that, I'll put the corn on, then I'll be done."

"That's what's up. I would've come through and helped you, cuz. How long have my future wife been here?"

"They got here not too long before you. So, you telling me that Kenzie is your future wife? She won't even give you the time of day," I laughed.

"Hell yeah, I'm claiming that! We have nothing but time and I'm going to give her that. She is worth the wait."

"Tell me how you figured out how to tell them apart. I had to remember what colors they were wearing."

"I'm gon' tell you this and you bet not forget it. Storm has a mole on the right side of her mouth. It's not very noticeable but I've studied her face every time I laid eyes on her, until I figured it out. Kane doesn't have that mole."

114

"You a bad muthafucka," I said giving Phantom a high five. "You just made my day. Run inside and get that last pan of meat. It's getting hot out here and I still need to take a shower."

Go handle your business. I'll handle the grill until you come back."

***

The barbeque was in full swing when I came back down from getting cleaned up. My backyard was packed and I was shocked, because it was only supposed to be the team and their families. *Who invited all these extra muthafuckas to my shit?* I wondered as I stepped out the door.

"Heyyyy, Khaos!"

I turned toward the voice and my blood started boiling when I saw my ex, Erica, sitting in a chair close to the door. Scanning the yard for Phantom, I spotted him on the other side of the pool with MaKenzie. Ignoring Erica, I took a step in the direction my cousin stood, and she grabbed me by my arm.

"You not gonna speak to me?" she asked with an attitude.

"What's up? Now get ya hands off me. Who told you to come here, Erica?"

"I heard you were having a get-together and was told to come through. Is it a problem?"

Walking away from her ass without replying, I made it to Phantom after passing through, speaking to whoever shouted out to me. My mood was fucked up because half of these muthafuckas were only there to eat and drink for free. It wasn't what I had in mind at all. Everybody knew I didn't like many at my crib.

"Cuz, how the fuck did all these muthafuckas know about this get-together?" I asked when I stood in front of Phantom.

"You know I had to find that shit out myself. Haze muthafuckin' ass told his damn baby mama and the bitch took the liberty to spread the word. I already told him what I thought about it and he chewed her ass out. She got in her feelings and left. I made the announcement that nobody is allowed inside the crib. Let's just have a good time and if shit goes left, we put their asses out of this bitch."

"Erica's ass is already trying to be on good bullshit. I don't want to be in the same breathing space as that bitch. As a matter of fact, she has to go," I said turning back toward the house.

Erica was no longer sitting by the door of the patio. I did a quick scan of the perimeter and she was nowhere in sight. Calming down a bit, I headed to the table and made me a double shot of Hennessy. The aroma of food hit my nostrils and I didn't have to think twice about fixing a hefty plate before I started drinking. As I sat and ate alone at the table, my gate was pushed open and in walked my lovely mother.

Standing to my feet, I waved her over and she looked around as she made her way to where I stood. My mother Kimille was beautiful, just like my aunt Karla. Seeing her in the multi-color maxi dress, with her freshly done toes peeping out of her pink sandals. Her hair was pinned to the top of her head.

"Hey, baby," my mother said as she wrapped her arms around my waist. "You know I don't do your little get-togethers. The weed is about to be thick and I want no parts of any of that. I came to see you, get a plate, and take my black ass home."

Phantom and MaKenzie walked over and he introduced her to my mother after hugging and kissing her cheek. Layla ran over and once again, she was picked up and coddled by my mother. After giving her many hugs and kisses, she turned to me and Phantom with fire in her eyes.

"Why is this baby here, Xavier? You know this isn't an environment she should be in."

"The festivities haven't started as of yet, Millie. I put everything on hold until you got here so I wouldn't have to beat yo' body for swinging on me."

"Now you know you're talking crazy. Where's my sister?"

Just as she asked, Auntie Karla walked out the house with a wrapped plate in her hand. "I'm right here and ready to get out of here. These fools about to start smoking those tweeds."

116

"Hey, beautiful, looking like me," my mama said, smiling at her sister.

"How you doing, mini-me? Have you seen the other beautiful twins running around here?"

"Nawl, you mean to tell me my boys done went out and got them a set of twins to get involved with?" my mama laughed.

Auntie Karla laughed as she looked around before noticing Kenzie standing by Phantom's side. "Oh, here's one of them. Where's your sister, Kenzie?"

Kenzie smiled and pointed to the lounge chair on the other side of the pool, where Kayla was relaxing with her shoes off. I followed her gaze and left the group to bring her back to meet my mother. When I stood before her, Kayla raised her sunglasses and looked up at me.

"I would like you to meet my mother. Can you come over for a few minutes?"

"Khaos, why would I be meeting your mother? Miss Karla already thinks we have something going on and that's far from the truth. I don't want your mother to think the same."

"Come on, nah. It's not even like that. She is talking to your sister now and Aunt Karla mentioned the two of you were twins, so she wants to meet you before she heads out."

I could see the hesitation in Kayla's movement, but she slowly swung her legs around and slipped her feet into her sandals. Reaching my hand out to help her up, I thought she was going to refuse, but she allowed me to assist her. When we got back to where my mama was, her eyes lit up and I knew then and there she approved of the woman I was smitten with.

"Hello, pretty," my mother said, giving Kayla a hug. One thing about our family, they loved to hug muthafuckas all the time.

"Nice to meet you. You're beautiful as well. Khaos must look like his daddy, because he doesn't have nothing on you," Kayla said, laughing.

"That's what many folks say, but that's my big baby. So, are you treating my son alright?"

Kayla glared at me and all I could do was hunch my shoulders. She rolled her eyes as she directed her attention back to my mother. Clearing her throat, Kayla rubbed the back of her neck before she answered the question.

"We're not an item. Khaos and I are only friends. I have a man back home in Chicago."

"Oh, y'all are not from Atlanta?"

"I have a home here and Chicago. I've lived here since I was younger, up until my grandmother passed away two years ago. Atlanta is home, Chicago is where my brother is. You can say, I have the best of both worlds."

My mother nodded her head in approval, and she had a gleam in her eye I knew all too well. Her ass was plotting. The moment was coming to an end, but this wouldn't be the last time they would see the Bennett twins. Both my mama and aunt loved to play matchmaker, but I never fell for their shenanigans.

"That's very impressive and I'm glad the two of you move together. There's nothing like sisterly love. Make sure your bond stays tight forever," Kimille said, turning to her son. "Kannon, fix ya mama a plate so I can get out of here. I know y'all are itching to, as you young folks say, turn up."

We all laughed as my mama tried to talk slang. Kayla stepped away and walked to the table to fix my mother's plate. When she came back, she handed her the plate and a bowl. Both were wrapped tightly in Saran Wrap.

"Who made the sides and banana pudding?" she asked.

"Both Kenzie and I cooked all the sides, and I made the banana pudding," Kayla replied.

"I'll let Kannon know if I approve. Usually I don't eat everybody's cooking, but I'm gonna give it a shot. Don't be strangers, ladies. I would love to spend a little time with you both. Enjoy the rest of your day, and I'll talk to you later, son."

Layla wiggled out of my mama's arms and hurried over to her daddy. Instead of hugging her father goodbye, she went directly to Kenzie and then showed Phantom love afterwards. If I noticed the exchange, I knew everyone else did too, but no one said a word. Tiff was in for a rude awakening if that lil girl started loving on Storm.

Meesha

Chapter 14

MaKenzie

Soon as Phantom and Khaos' mothers left the yard, it seemed as if everyone was waiting for the moment to present itself. The air got thick as fuck and I was right in the midst of it all. We smoked and drank while music blared from the speakers. Some of the females stripped out of their clothes baring their skimpy swimsuits before diving in the pool. Even though Khaos was upset about the extra bodies at first, things were going very well for all in attendance.

"Storm, I want my money back," Khaos said, coming to the table I was sitting at. "Let's run these cards and put a wager on it."

"Depends on what you trying to play."

"We gon' hit this Texas Hold 'Em, a hunnid a hand."

"I'm down for the cause. Poker isn't my game of choice, but it's definitely a game of chance. Who else is down?" I asked.

"Let me ask seven more muthafuckas, then I'll go in the crib and grab the set." Khaos turned his back and I started laughing. "What's funny?" he asked, facing me.

"You must be the poker master, that's why you chose that particular game. It's cool, I'm familiar with it and I'm up for the challenge. Go do what you gotta do and I'll be right here waiting for your return."

Gathering more people to play, Khaos grabbed the poker set and came back to the yard. Phantom, Killah, Haze, Dreux, his boy Jax, Shoota, and Jax's brother Snipe joined the table and the game was underway. Kayla stood beside Khaos, blowing a spiff of Za as she watched him deal the cards. There was some big money on the table, and I was ready to win that shit. Scony taught me how to play the game of poker many years prior and I was about to hustle their ass once again.

Khaos won the first hand with two pair, going head-to-head with Shoota. He raised the pot by two hundred and got his ass popped. Everybody at the table had won some type of money except me. I was losing purposely and the money I started with was dwindling fast. We had been playing for over an hour, but I was getting up with some of my money, fuck that.

"How much money you got over there, Storm? I can hit you with something to keep you in the game longer," Phantom said lowly.

"Don't worry about it, if I lose, I lose. This ain't shit to a big fish. Play your shit to win and leave my coins to me."

"Aight, playa. I was just trying to help your stubborn ass out," Phantom said, sitting back in his chair. I didn't bother replying because I was praying for some good cards to come my way.

Khaos distributed the cards and I took a look at mine. Keeping my expression blank, I smiled on the inside because I had pocket queens. I had to play this shit cool. It was my time to lure a few of these muthafuckas in. All the players wanted to see the flop and paid into the pot. When it was my turn, I hesitated before reluctantly throwing my chips in.

Khaos revealed the flop and there was a queen of hearts, nine of clubs, and a ten of spades. I knew someone was bound to have a run for a straight, but I wasn't worried. Shoota threw his cards in, Jax tossed in his bet, raising two hundred dollars. Dreux called and so did everyone else. When it was my turn, I bit my lip and glanced around the table nervously before adding my chips to the pot.

When the turn card was revealed, it was a jack of diamonds and I knew somebody had a fucking straight. There was a strong chance my three of a kind queens were going to break me. Cards were being thrown to the center of the table and that left Phantom, Khaos, and me still in the hand. The betting began with Khaos raising the pot by three hundred dollars. Phantom went behind him and called. I didn't hesitate a minute to add my money too.

"Oh, shyt! We got a muthafuckin' game," Phantom screamed.

The river card was turned and my eyes lit up, but I made sure to suppress it quickly. The queen of diamonds stared in my face and there was no way I would lose this hand. Glaring at Khaos, I waited for him to make his move because I knew he was about to call himself, forcing me to fold. Little did he know, it wasn't about to happen. I was ready to push the five hundred dollars I had left into the pot.

"You're playing a grown man's game over there, Storm. I hope you ready to get the fuck up and take a dip in the pool."

This nigga didn't learn shit from me hustling his ass at the bowling alley. Something should've told him I wasn't the average female he was used to. Kayla already knew he was about to be wearing egg yolk on his face because she smirked at me and I nodded my head.

"I've come too far to give up. Do whatever you gon' do, fam, because I think I got yo' ass," Phantom said with confidence. "Storm don't know what she's doing on that end so, I'm not too worried about her. But yo' ass, let's go."

I loved how both of them assumed I didn't know what I was doing. My granny always said when you assume, you make an ass outta ya'self. I was about to make that saying come to life soon as they put their money on the table.

"I'm raising this shit five bills," Khaos said, throwing his chips into the middle of the table.

"Bet, I'm right behind you," Phantom quickly said as he placed his bet.

"I guess you pushed me all in," I smiled wickedly.

Dreux sat back, cheesing his ass off because other than Kayla, he was the only other person that knew I lived for a good game of poker. Phantom turned his cards over revealing a jack and an eight, giving him a queen high straight. Khaos stood and slammed his cards down on the table as he showed his jack and king giving him the win over Phantom. He reached for the pile of chips and I stood and laughed.

"Aht-aht, homie. Don't touch that because it belongs to me."

"I won this pot, baby girl. There's no way you beat me out. Shid, ya man over there couldn't even beat me." Khaos started moving the chips toward him when I turned my cards over without breaking eye contact.

"If I remember correctly, four of a kind beats anything that's not a straight flush or royal flush. That means, my four queens smashed the shit out of your straight. Let me get those five bands outta ya, nigga," I smiled.

"Damn!" Jax jumped up, laughing. "She hustled the shit out of yo' ass, Khaos! I can't believe a woman fucked you up at yo' own game."

"I told y'all last night and I'll say it again right now, stop underestimating these two muthafuckas," Dreux laughed heartily, moving his finger back and forth in me and Kayla's direction. "They are niggas just like us, they just wear weave and got bangin' bodies. I'm taking my money and leaving this shit alone."

Kayla started counting Dreux's remaining chips and handed him his money. She went around the table and when she got to me, she counted out forty-nine hundred dollars in one hundred-dollar bills. Counting off a grand, I handed the bills to her and stood to my feet.

"When you're ready to lose again, get my number from ya boy and I'll be there with bells on," I said, walking to the table to fix a plate.

"Storm, hell nawl! You are not about to walk away with my money again!" Khaos said angrily.

"She won that shit fair and square, cuz. You can't get mad." Phantom laughed but he was lowkey pissed too, he just didn't want to show it. His boys were having a field day with the shit as they continued to roast both of them about losing to a female.

I ate my food as somebody started singing and they sounded like a howling cat sitting on a fence in an alley. Straining my neck to see what the hell was going on, words to the song was rolling on the large projection screen and I wanted it to stop. Karaoke was in full effect and I was all for it. I hurried to finish eating because I wanted in. Making a stiff drink, I threw the empty plate in the garbage and made my way across the yard.

Searching through the song book, I looked for the one song I loved and found it. Daniel Caesar's "Best Part," featuring H.E.R. was what I wanted to sing to bring some sultry shit to this party. The folks that had been at the mic didn't sound good at all, and I had to put an end to it. I added my name to the list and there was two people before me. Standing waiting for my turn to come up, I toned out the screeching pounding through the speakers, but it was a difficult task.

"You trying to sing, I see," Phantom said, walking up to me.

"Trying? Stand there and watch me act up. Somebody has to entertain y'all, because these muthafuckas ain't," I laughed.

"I'm gon' be right here checkin' you out."

They were calling for the female who was on the list before me, but she waved them off and decided not to participate. My name was called and I walked to the mic. When the music started, Phantom walked up and grabbed the other mic.

"What are you doing?" I asked.

"This is a duet, baby. Let's shine together. You better blow this shit too. Don't make me look bad," he smirked. The track was started over and all of a sudden, I got nervous. "You got this, come on. Start it again, fam," Phantom yelled. The music started and I closed my eyes and bellowed out the words.

Oh, hey
You don't know, babe
When you hold me
And kiss me slowly
It's the sweetest thing
And it don't change
If I had it my way
You would know that you are

Phantom joined me with the chorus, and I stopped singing completely because his voice didn't match his hard demeanor at all. That shit had my kitty tingling and I was mesmerized and couldn't take my eyes off him. When he sang the next verse, my mouth hung wide open and I could've sworn my tongue was wagging with saliva on the tip.

It's this sunrise
And those brown eyes, yes
You're the one that I desire
When I wake up
And then we make love

It makes me feel so nice
You're my water when I'm stuck in the desert
You're the Tylenol I take when my head hurts
You're the sunshine of my life
I forgot to join him with the chorus, and he laughed but kept singing as he pulled me into his body. Forcing the words out my mouth, I caught back up with him, but there was something in the atmosphere as he sang that song. I was lost in his being and I didn't like at all. Breaking away from his embrace, I placed the mic on the table and walked away. Phantom kept singing and I felt his eyes on my back, but I didn't stop until I was inside the house and in the bathroom.

Snatching a couple paper towels from the roll on the sink, I turned on the cold water and wiped my face vigorously. I was hot as hell and didn't quite know why. Yes, I did, it was that damn Phantom with his fine ass. There was no way I should've been lusting over him, knowing I didn't want any type of relationship outside of sex. The way he looked at me while he sang, Phantom had the power to make my hardcore ass fall hard for him.

Rapid knocks on the door brought me out of my thoughts. I turned the water off and took a deep breath. Opening the door, I came face-to-face with Kayla. The way my sister stared at me, I knew she was about to be on some good bullshit.

"What the hell was that about?" she asked with her hand on her hip.

"I don't know what you're talking about." Trying to walk out the door, Kayla blocked my exit by placing her hand on the frame. "Move, Kayla!"

"No. Tell me what's wrong with you."

"There's nothing wrong, sis. I just had to use the bathroom, okay? It was nothing behind it."

"Let me find out you let that man shake you up in front of all those people. Your face is flustered. I know he got you feeling some type of way, because the way he held you while singing into your soul, yo' ass damn near passed out."

126

Kayla laughed and I didn't find anything funny. If she saw my reaction, I knew everyone else did too. It was time for me to leave, but I needed to go back outside to grab my phone from the table by the projector.

"I'm ready to go. I have to get my phone and then we're leaving," I said, pushing my way pass her arm.

As I rushed to the backyard, I could see everybody staring at the projector. My eyes followed suit and there was a video showing on the screen. A black man was being apprehended by the police with his hands handcuffed behind him and the white officer was kneeling with his knee in the back of his neck. I knew if the video was being broadcasted, nothing good was going to come from it.

Easing out of the door slowly, I could hear the guy telling the officer he couldn't breathe. There were witnesses yelling at the officer to get his knee off his neck and kept repeating, "He can't breathe."

The officer in turn said, "If he's speaking, he's fine." The man was crying out in pain and the officer had his knee in his neck for eight minutes and forty-six seconds.

The sight before me broke my heart, but when he called out for his mama and said, "They gon' kill me," I cried a river.

"See, this the type of shit that will make me fuck a muthafucka up! When will this stop!" Shoota raged.

"These cops are too comfortable with doing this type of shit! Look at that nigga with his hands in his pockets like it's nothing!" Phantom screamed. "I see another movement coming. This shit is pathetic and we can't let it go on another day!"

"He's not moving y'all! Oh my God, he's dead," I cried openly.

Phantom turned in my direction and rushed to my side. I was bawling my eyes out, but I couldn't stop watching what was happening on the screen. Gathering me in his arms, Phantom rubbed my back while I cried. An ambulance pulled up and the EMT walked over and checked the guy's pulse, but how, when the fuckin' police still had his knee on his neck! I knew the guy was gone because he wasn't moving at all.

The EMT brought out a stretcher and the police officer finally stood to his feet. Two of the officers dragged the guy's body toward the stretcher and threw him onto it. There was no attempt at saving his life. No oxygen, chest compressions, or anything. They just wheeled his body to the ambulance and chugged him inside. That man was murdered right before our eyes and the police didn't see anything wrong with it.

The video ended and the outrage in the yard was at an all-time high. No one wanted to party anymore. We stood around following the story on every social media platform as many helped clean up. I couldn't get the sight of the guy taking his last breath out of my head and I was exhausted.

"I'm about to leave," I said to Phantom. "This has drained the fuck out of me." Tears ran down my face and my heart ached as if the guy was someone I knew personally. He could've been my brother!

"Are you gon' be alright?" Phantom asked.

Shaking my head no, I swiped at my eyes, but the tears kept coming. "They killed that man, Phantom! Why do our black men keep having to go through this? We have seen this far too many times. They don't care about us as black men and women! To make it so bad, nothing is going to happen to those fuckin' pigs!"

"I know, Storm. You are right about everything you've said. It's happening too often and it's like we'll never get equal justice in this country. And they had a problem with Colin Kaepernick kneeling during the National Anthem. This is why he did that shit. We as a people, have to fight for change."

"Breonna Taylor and Tatiana Jefferson were in the comfort of their own homes when the police killed them. Eric Garner was killed when a police officer choked him out over selling loose squares. Sandra Bland was murdered. I don't give a fuck what no-body says, she didn't commit suicide. Why would she? Her bail was only five hundred muthafuckin' dollars! Ahmaud Arbery was out jogging and got gunned down by two white men and one used to wear a badge, they didn't arrest the muthafuckas until the video went viral seventy- four days later!" I was mad, hurt, numb. You name it, I was it.

"I know, Storm."

Phantom held me tight and I couldn't function. I was tired of being quiet watching this shit happen daily to our people. We didn't deserve any of the things that was happening with us.

"We can't go to Walmart and look at the guns they sell without getting killed. What's the use of having a conceal and carry license, if we can't carry a weapon without being shot as we reach for our identification? I'm tired of this mess! They don't give a fuck about us!"

"Calm down. I feel your pain and I'm pissed too. I understand everything you're saying and it's nothing but the truth." Jax walked over after hearing me speak my piece. I was sniffling as I dug in my purse for a Kleenex.

"I understand all the shit you're saying, but why isn't this same outrage voiced when there's black-on-black crime? Y'all go through this shit every time a white police officer kills somebody black. Have that same energy when we killing each other," Jax declared.

Phantom's jaw clenched at the same moment my blood started boiling. This nigga had the nerve to be talking about black-on-black crime when that wasn't even relevant. We were in a state of turmoil and our whole race was being hunted by racist ass police.

"Why the fuck would you bring up black-on-black crime?" Phantom's voice boomed. "It's niggas like you that want to try and rectify what these muthafuckas are doing to us. You are part of the fuckin' problem, nigga."

"Don't get mad at me! I said what the fuck I said. We kill each other every day and there's no protest about that. But the minute something like this happens, y'all wanna start talking 'Black Lives Matter.' Get the fuck outta here with that bullshit," Jax had the nerve to say.

Phantom lunged at Jax and grabbed him by the collar. It took Khaos, Shoota, Dreux, and Killah to pull him off that man. His eyes turned red and I saw firsthand that he could really hurt Jax badly.

Stepping in to defuse the situation, I placed my hand on his arm and he glanced over at me and his facial expression softened.

"Let him go. Everybody has a right to their opinion. It doesn't matter how stupid he sounds, you must let this shit go. Jax won't be the first nor the last person who thinks differently than most. Like you said, he is part of the problem and he won't understand until the shit happens to him. Whooping his ass won't stop police brutality. Arguing with him won't solve what's going on in the world. Let him go, Phantom."

Phantom released Jax by shoving him in the chest, making him stumble backwards a couple feet. Shoota grabbed Jax by the arm so he wouldn't fall on his ass, but he snatched away. Straightening his collar of his shirt, Jax glared at Phantom but shook his head as he backed up towards the gate.

"I'm gon' let you have that because I know the situation has you heated, but don't ever put yo' muthafuckin' hands on me again. You didn't even know that nigga and you ready to beat me up for telling the truth."

"Jax, that's yo' truth, not mine," Phantom said, taking a step in his direction. "You're not wrong about black-on-black crime, but that is not the issue! These pigs have been doing this shit way before our time and continue to do it. It's open season for black people, man. At first, they were targeting men. Now, they don't give a fuck! You saw that shit right along with us, that was murder!"

Phantom stopped moving toward Jax and waved his hand. He grabbed my hand without saying anything and led me through the house. We exited Khaos' house and headed to his whip. I looked up and Kayla was coming out of the house with Khaos on her heels. They exchanged pleasantries and my sister walked to her car.

"I'll call you later, sis. I'm going to ride with Phantom."

"Don't do anything I wouldn't do." Kayla smirked as she climbed in her car.

The day started out great but ended leaving a bad aftertaste in my mouth. The world is about to go from sugar to shit behind this murder. There's no way we as black people would allow this one to get swept under the rug.

130

Chapter 15

Phantom

I had to get the fuck away from Jax before I split his shit to the white meat. It's a damn shame we as black people were being hunted like wolves, but to have another nigga bring up some shit that was irrelevant than a muthafucka to take the focus off the problem at hand, had me wanting to beat his ass. Kenzie was only in the passenger seat of my ride because I pulled her along when I left Khaos' crib. I knew for sure she was going to put up a fight, but she didn't.

"Where are we going?" she asked after I'd been driving for about ten minutes.

"I don't know, to be honest. Would you mind if I stopped by my mama's crib for a minute? I need to pick up Layla since I didn't stay at the barbeque."

"No, it's cool. So, are you a single dad?"

Driving without responding for a minute, I glanced over at Kenzie, shaking my head. "Nah, I may be soon though. Layla's mama is a piece of work."

"Are you saying she's a piece of work because things aren't good between the two of y'all right now?" Kenzie was asking questions in order to see what position Tiff played in my life. It was cool because I had nothing to hide, and what me and Tiff had was nothing more than two parents trying to coexist for our daughter.

"Things haven't been good with us for years. Me and Tiff will never be an item again in life. Even though she has a man, Tiff always has a problem with any woman I'm spending time with. She is on a power trip right now because I shot her nigga the other day."

"You shot him?" Kenzie asked, laughing. "What made you do that, if there's nothing going on between y'all?"

"That muthafucka was whoopin' her ass in front of Layla. I don't give a damn what they have going on, but they won't be doing the shit in front of my daughter. I knocked his ass out and he reached for his pistol and I shot his ass in both of his legs. Took my daughter and left."

"Wait! You shot him and let him live another day to come back at you? What type of nigga are you? That's not how you do shit in these streets today. He's going to be on your head soon as he's healed. You created a problem when all you had to do was put that nigga out his misery when you had a chance."

"I know the code and I'll be ready for whatever he brings my way," I said, pulling into my mama's driveway. "I couldn't shoot that nigga to kill him, because I didn't want it to traumatize Layla."

Soon as I cut the engine, a car pulled up behind mine and Tiffany jumped out of her car. This was her typical tactic whenever she was stalking to get in my business. She must've already tried her hand at seeing Layla through my mama and waited for me to pull up to get in my face about the situation.

"Who the fuck is that?" Kenzie asked as Tiff banged on my driver's window.

"That's Tiff. Don't say anything, let me handle this. Get out, ring the doorbell and go inside. I'll be in behind you momentarily." Kenzie opened the door and Tiff ran around the front of my car and got in her face. Kenzie stood without saying anything and I jumped out of the car before things escalated too far.

"Who the fuck is you? Do you know Phantom is my baby's father?"

"Did you know I don't care? See, you are the one that procreated with that man, not me. For you to come at me with the bullshit, you must be outta yo' mind," Kenzie said calmly.

"Nah, you are the one that's gonna learn today that Phantom is off limits. He don't need no other bitch, when he got me."

"Bitch, you sound stupid as hell! I just got out of this man's car, so obviously he wanted me there. Fuck all that, what's your purpose for addressing me and not your man?"

Tiffany stood there looking dumb, so I approached and she turned to me with a scowl on her face. I wanted her to focus on me and less on Kenzie, because I knew for a fact, she didn't stand a chance against Storm. To be honest, I was trying to save her ass at the moment.

"Look, Tiff, you and I know me and you have not been together as a couple for years. Why are you trying to make this out of something it's not? First of all, she don't have nothing to do with how you feel about me. Shit, I don't for that matter. Second of all, walking up on her wasn't necessary. I should've been the one you came to if there was a problem, not her."

Tiff clenched her fist at her side and swung backwards, barely hitting Kenzie in the face. That's all it took for Storm to emerge and put the foo flops on her ass. I let Storm fuck Tiff up for a few minutes, before I grabbed her around the waist and got her off of my baby mama. Tiff was leaking from the mouth and she had a knot on the side of her head bigger than a golf ball. It must've happened when Storm banged her head on the concrete.

"I'm cool, Phantom. I showed the bitch I'm not to be played with," Kenzie said, trying to pry my arms off her. She stepped over Tiff and headed toward the house before doing an about-face. "Next time you see me, I don't care where that may be, cross the street. What you received today, was just a taste of what I can actually do to your bum ass, bitch."

As I helped Tiff to her feet, my mama was walking out the front door. She stepped to the side so Kenzie could enter and pointed inside to Layla who had followed her outside. I knew the lecture was coming and I was ready for it. Surprisingly, my mama didn't address me. Instead, she had some choice words for Tiff.

"Didn't I tell your ass to get away from my house, Tiffany? A hard head makes a soft ass and you finally got a woman that wasn't for your bullshit. Now, get in your car and get the fuck away from here."

"It's all good, I'll see that bitch again. She caught me off guard but next time, I'll be ready."

Tiff pushed past me and stomped to her car. Watching as she pulled off burning rubber, I turned around and made my way up the walkway.

"Kenzie whooped her ass! You better tell that damn girl to stay away from her. She didn't play with her, not one bit! Tiff came over talking about she was scheduled to pick up Layla. I told her you hadn't said anything to me about any of that and sent her on her way."

"She was telling a boldfaced lie, Ma. I haven't talked to Tiff at all. This is not the time for her to be fuckin' with me. Did you hear about the man in Minnesota who was killed by the police?"

"It's all over the news. They didn't have to do him like that! All over a counterfeit twenty-dollar bill! This shit is ridiculous. I hope they convict every one of those police. I'm tired of them killing our people and getting away with it. There will be a protest going on tomorrow and I know people are going to be there in droves."

"I'm about to make it happen, because I'll be there too. Will you keep Layla for a few days? I can't be silent about this. We have to stand together in order to make a change."

Both me and my mama walked into her house and into the living room. Layla and Kenzie were sitting on the couch watching CNN. I really didn't want my daughter watching what was going on in the world, but I didn't want to shelter her from it either.

"Daddy, the police killed that man," Layla said, running towards me full speed. "He called for his mama because he knew he was gonna die. That was wrong for that policeman to do that to him."

My heart swelled because my baby didn't understand what was actually going on. The way she was crying hurt my soul. Her little body was shivering, and I knew she was crying from the image she saw on the television.

"Baby, don't cry. Yes, it was very wrong what happened to him," I said, stroking her back to calm her.

"What if something like that happens to you? The police are supposed to protect us, not kill us," Layla wailed.

"It won't happen to me, Lay. You don't have to worry about that, baby."

Kissing my daughter on her cheek, I sat on the sofa next to Kenzie and watched the news segment that was on. The news reporter was talking about the video and the guy succumbed from the restraint on his neck. The police claimed the individual, identified as forty-six-year-old George Floyd was resisting arrest. Which was an outright lie, because there was a second video that showed what transpired from beginning to end.

"They need to be locked the fuck up! The Asian cop is standing there, trying to block the person filming, but didn't do a great job of it. He could've stopped what happened to George and did nothing except stand there while his fellow officer literally killed him!"

The news segment went to the live footage of people gathering in the street, outraged about what happened. "People are gathering in the streets and they are chanting, 'No justice, no peace! Black Lives Matter!' I believe this is about to go in a whole different direction. I agree with the people, this was murder. Something has to be done," the reporter stated.

I watched as the crowd became thick in the streets of Minneapolis, and being there was something I wanted to do. Looking down at my daughter, I realized I needed to march and protest so I could be part of the change in this movement. My mind was made up, I had to get things in motion to get to Minnesota.

"We have to go to Minnesota," Storm said as if she was reading my mind. "Do you have access to a plane? If we're going, we have to head out before it gets hectic. What we don't want to do is wait. We have to get into that state before things go awry, because we will be denied access. Tonight, is the time to go and show out. Are you down?"

"Hell yeah, I'm with the shits," I said, pulling my phone from my pocket. I hit the name I was looking for and listened while the phone rang.

"You see this shit on TV, man? This shit is bogus as hell."

"I see it, Tim. You ready to roll? We gon' need your jet so we can get there with no problems. You know how we're about to roll."

"Damn right! I'm about to get the pilot on the line to make sure the jet is gassed up. We gon' aim for seven o'clock, so be at the strip because when the clock strikes seven, I'm leaving with or without you. Bring whomever, because we can be at least twenty deep, I have at least ten rolling with me."

"Aight, bet. See you at seven." Ending the call, I looked up at my mama. She already knew not to try and talk me out of going. Instead, she nodded her head and reached for Layla.

"Be careful, baby."

I kissed my daughter on the forehead, expressing my love for her. Storm was already on the phone texting and with every ping, I knew the responses were lucrative. I had to make sure I came back to Atlanta alive to raise my daughter.

Chapter 16

MaKayla

Seeing the video at Khaos' house, had me mad as hell. I couldn't get the vision of the officer with his knee in that man's neck out of my mind. After taking a shower, I lounged on my bed with a bowl of fruit as music blared from the Bluetooth speaker. K'Jon's "On the Ocean" was playing and I closed my eyes as I grooved to the soulful beat. My phone rang, interrupting the song and I instantly got an attitude. After all of his whining, Conte finally decided to dial my number.

I should've let it ring until the voicemail picked up, but I decided against it. Hearing what he had to say was better done at that time, rather than later. Breathing through my nose, I accepted the call before I got up and headed to the kitchen. A drink was much needed to keep my attitude at bay.

"What's up, Conte?" I asked as I descended the stairs.

"Why haven't I heard from you, Kayla? You left last week and this the first time we've talked." I listened, but didn't utter a vowel, why should I? The nigga called everybody but me when I stepped out of my house. "Hello?"

"I'm still here, continue," I responded nonchalantly.

"Answer the question. Why haven't I heard from you?"

"Conte, you should already know the answer already. You had the same capability to call, but instead, you picked everybody except me to voice your problem with."

"I didn't have a choice. Kayla, you walked out and didn't look back. Basically, you told me to kiss yo' ass without voicing it out loud."

"You didn't have a choice? Is that what you just said out of your mouth? If you know anything about me, you would know discussing me with anyone other than myself is a no-no. I should've been the first person you called when you wanted to get shit off your chest. Instead, I get a call from my brother trying to check me about my relationship."

Conte was quiet for a moment and I took the opportunity to pour a hefty amount of tequila in a glass. Opening the refrigerator, I added pineapple mango juice to my glass and made my way back up the stairs. Planting my foot on the first step, Conte's voice boomed through the phone.

"What the fuck are you doing, Kayla?"

"I'm walking to my bedroom, if you don't mind. Lower your tone when you're talking to me and explain why you had to tell not only Scony my business, but also Monty. What, you got him watching my every move now?"

"I don't have anyone watching you! Yo' muthafuckin' ass left here without a care in the world. So, are you saying we are over? And don't take too damn long to respond either."

I chuckled, crawling onto my king-sized bed. "That's one I can easily answer. You told me we were over when you gave me an ultimatum. To be honest, our relationship should've been over a long time ago. Damn near every time you went out of town, I received a text from your phone. You chose the stupidest hoes to fuck with me, Conte. They wanted me to know what you were doing when you were out of my presence."

"Kayla, you don't have to lie to get out of this shit!"

"I've never been a liar, there's no reason for me to do such a thing. The shit has been going on for about a year, but I never spoke on it because I knew the day to expose your ass would present itself," I said, taking a sip from my drink.

"There's Anita from Detroit. She felt the need to contact me about the abortion you forced her to have at two and a half months pregnant. Then, we have Monifah in Memphis that was upset because you wouldn't move her to Chicago, because you wanted to keep hiding her from what she said was me. Let's not forget the fact you told her you and I was over. Oh, I can't leave out Santa. She was the one that knew how to keep her mouth shut, until you uttered those three words that swelled her heart."

Conte was quiet as hell when I exposed what I knew, but I didn't expect him to say anything in response. It felt good to get that shit out, because his ass was going hard for a relationship he hadn't honored for the past year. He was going all-out to make me the bad one in the situation, when he was the head villain.

"You have nothing to say now, huh?" I asked calmly.

"If I did any of the things you claim, why say something now?" Conte asked angrily.

"There was no reason for me to bring the shit to you. I may be young, but at the same time, I didn't and still don't need a nigga. I chose to accept what we had and let you think you were being the playa you were destined to be. See, I knew I was going to get an opportunity to make you eat the food you dished out. Now, let's see how you gon' feel when I fuck just because."

"Kayla, I'm sorry! That's what men do and I didn't love any of them hoes. I love you!" Conte started yelling and I laughed.

"Love is one thing you didn't have for me and I've known for some time. Sitting back, I took in how you treated me and ran with it. I didn't give a damn what you did with the other bitches because that was your problem, not mine. My focus was set on what you did when you were with me. But since you're making it seem like I left your ass high and dry, now you know your actions played a major part in all of this."

"I apologize, damn!"

"Well, your apology is not accepted, Conte. You can keep the house. I won't be back to Chicago anytime soon. I'm kind of glad we decided to hold off on having kids. It wouldn't surprise me if you had a seed or two out there you've kept hidden. We have nothing more to argue about. Both of us can walk away from this without any worries."

"You not gon' treat me like I'm the bitch in this relationship!"

"You portrayed yourself in that manner and I let you have it. Enjoy your life, Conte. You had a good one and decided to abuse your privilege. I didn't leave you alone back then, but it's a wrap now. You needed side bitches and I needed a muthafucka that would do right by me. You were into hiding these hoes to keep me. I'm into giving yo seat to the next nigga. You're free to do whatever you like and that goes both ways. I'm about to have the time of my life being a single woman. Be easy, pimp."

139

Ending the call, I continued to sip from my glass and the music started playing again. I ran the song back and listened to it from the beginning without a care in the world. About fifteen minutes later, my phone rang again, and it was Kenzie on the other end.

"Hey, Twin. What are you and Phantom up to? It can't be much because you're on the phone with me."

"Girl, I had to knock his baby mama upside the head, but I'll tell you about that on the plane. You down to travel in about two hours?"

"Hell yeah, where we going?" I asked, sitting up.

"We're heading to Minnesota to protest the shit that happened to George Floyd. Be ready in an hour and strap the fuck up."

Kenzie hung up and I was too excited to march for the cause. My sister was on some other shit, because she made it a point to tell me to strap up. As I got my arsenal together, my phone rang back-to-back, but I knew it was Conte and he could kiss my ass because I was done with his bullshit.

Chapter 17

Nicassy

Heat sent me on a blank mission, and I was going to kill a man based on false pretense. I should've known there was something shady about the job he sent me on, because he didn't want me to tell anybody. Keeping my mouth closed wasn't hard because I hadn't been fucking with the twins for a long while anyway. Telling Stone the truth was what I'd been beating myself up about since I hung up on Heat's ass. Playing his game should've been my move, but I was mad and allowed the words I was thinking to flow from my lips.

Pacing back and forth across the floor of the bedroom I shared with Stone, trying to come up with the best way to tell Stone the real reason I entered his life. When we first met at Club Onyx, my mission was to slip him a Mickey and lure him out of the club to kill him. But my plans changed because his entourage was too thick for me to get close to him, so I had to find another way to get his attention. I made it rain on the stripper that was on stage and with every drop of the beat, I made my ass clap while standing directly in front of Stone.

There were many strippers frolicking to the group of men, but I felt eyes on me. I smiled to myself because I had a feeling Stone was giving my ass his undivided attention. After tucking the last of the bills I had into the stripper's G-string, I downed the alcohol left in my glass and headed for the exit. By the time I got to my car, Stone was calling out behind me and I had hooked his ass without opening my mouth.

I was only supposed to be in Houston for two days, but it turned into almost a year after I got comfortable with the two of us spending a lot of time together. Stone let me into his world, and I took the opportunity to see if I would catch him in the bullshit Heat claimed he was into. While going out with him to collect money from his tenants at the many properties he owned, I learned Stone was all about money. He also owned a carwash, barbershop, and later I found out he also owned Club Onyx.

Heat portrayed Stone as a pedophile and that was far from the truth. If he wasn't checking on his businesses and working, he was on the phone conducting more business. His sisters and his parents were the main priorities in his life. The ringing of my phone brought me out of my thoughts, and I rushed to the other side of the room and realized it was my secondary phone I usually left in the car. I forgot I even brought it inside and wanted to kick myself for slipping.

"Hey, bro," I answered drily.

"Nicassy, what's up, baby girl? You've been missing in action, what's going on with ya?" Scony asked on the other end.

"Yeah, I've been taking some much-needed time to myself. I've been meaning to call and check on you, but it slips my mind."

"Come on now, sis. It's been damn near a year since I've heard from you. Coming by the house has never been a problem when it comes to us, you'll always be family. Tell me what's really going on, because that shit you just said ain't cutting it."

Taking a seat on the edge of the bed, I took a deep breath because Scony could always tell when me or his sisters were lying to him. Nine times out of ten, he talked to Kenzie and he knew her side of the conversation we had days ago. I may as well tell him mine.

"Scony, you have always welcomed me into your home. I'm just not in Chicago anymore, that's the reason I haven't been by to see you."

"What do you mean you're not in Chicago anymore? When did we start keeping secrets? And that means the twins don't know your location either, because Kenzie didn't mention anything when I talked to her. Am I right?" he asked sternly.

"Yeah, you're right. Neither one of them knows my whereabouts. What else did Kenzie say when you talked to her?" I wanted to know if she smeared my name in the mud or not.

"Don't think you gon' get away from the questions I asked, Nicassy. I'm definitely coming back to that shit. To answer your question, Kenzie is the reason I'm calling, on top of not hearing from you for so long. She told me about the conversation the two of y'all had and I don't like that y'all are bumping heads. What's that about?"

"Since we've been working for Heat, it's like Kenzie is put on a pedestal and I'm just her sidekick. She takes that shit and runs with it and thinks shit is supposed to go her way or no way. We get paid the same amount of money, and she wants to be on a whole different level than me and Kayla. I'm tired of that shit for real. I shouldn't have to water myself down for her to shine."

"Sis, y'all been through too much for this petty shit. All you had to do was tell Kenzie how you felt when you had the chance. We're all we got and this shit needs to be hashed out. There's too much going on in the world for y'all to be bickering about nothing. When you get back to Atlanta, get together, hug and make up. I'm not getting in this shit, because it's something the two of y'all have to work out on your own."

I knew Scony was right, but Kenzie was too stuck in her ways to even talk to anyone rationally. It would end up being a bigger problem than before, because she felt she was always right. I was going to try and talk to her, but it wasn't going to be anytime soon. Whenever I felt the time was right, I'd make the call, but it wasn't going to be on Scony's terms.

"I'm not in Atlanta, so that's not going to happen. I'll give her a call though."

"With that being said, this brings us back to what's going on with you. Where the fuck is you, Nicassy?" Scony's voice elevated a few octaves and I knew he was upset.

"I'm on a job in Houston."

"How are you on a job and nobody knows where you are? That's not the way shit is usually handled with y'all. Somebody needs to know your location at all times, in case something goes wrong!"

"I was given specific orders not to tell anyone where I was and—"

"Specific orders from who? I know damn well the connect didn't put you out there like that!"

"It was a strange request, but I went along with it because there was a big paycheck behind it."

"You put your life in jeopardy for money? Tell me about the muthafuckin' assignment, Nicassy. You don't have to go into detail, but I need to know where the fuck you are, in case something goes wrong."

"I just wanted to get away and do something to keep myself occupied, so I took the damn job! Scony, I fell in love with the mark, okay? I was told the person I was sent to hit was a pedophile. I've been here almost a year and none of what I was told is true. His family is the best and so is he. I'm going to talk to him and come clean about everything."

Scony was quiet a minute before he sighed into the phone. "You are playing a dangerous game, Nicassy. I advise you to just pack up and abort the mission. There's no way he's going to forgive you for entering his life under false pretense. Coming from a man like myself, I would shoot yo' ass between the eyes and dispose of your body, and you would never be heard from again. Get the fuck out of there and don't say shit! I want an address now!"

"I'm at 31939 Maverick Way in Houston, Texas. The target's name is Stone on the streets." Hearing the alarm chirp was an indication Stone was home, and I had to get off the phone. "I have to go. I will text you the number to my other phone and I will keep in touch. Thanks for always being there, bro. I love you."

"Be careful, sis. I will fuck some shit up if something happens to you."

"I'm going to be alright. I promise."

Ending the call, I quickly sent Scony a text and shut the phone off, before going into the closet to hide the phone in one of my other purses. I climbed into the bed and picked up my iPad, just as Stone was entering the bedroom. He looked good enough to eat, standing in the doorway with his dress shirt and slacks on.

"Hey, baby," he said, walking in and unbuttoning his shirt.

"Hey." That's all I could muster up to say because my mind was on telling him about why I came to Texas nine months ago.

Diverting my eyes back to my iPad, Stone walked further into the room and sat on the edge of the bed and lifted my head with his finger.

"What's on your mind, baby? You look kind of down."

"I'm tired, that's all. How was your meeting?" I asked, trying to steer the conversation away from me.

He leaned over and planted a kiss on my lips before standing to his feet. Stone pulled the shirt from his body, exposing his muscular back. My kitty always purred whenever I saw his tatted body.

"The meeting went very well actually. I stopped to see Celeste today. Did you know she was pregnant?"

Hearing Stone bring up Celeste's pregnancy made my head snap in his direction quickly. Even though his sisters were grown, Stone was very protective over both of them, especially Celeste. He couldn't stand Joe, right along with the rest of us and wanted a reason to snatch his head from his neck.

"Yeah, I knew. It wasn't my place to say anything though, baby."

"No, no, no. That's not where I'm going with this, Angel." I cringed when he called me by the name my grandmother gave me when I was younger. Guilt set in as I sat back on the bed. "Celeste explained what's going on with her and Joe. I didn't agree with the way she's putting up with his bullshit, but I'm going to stay out of it until I need to fuck him up."

"That's a good choice. Celeste will realize how worthy she is and leave his trifling ass when the time is right. I already told her she's not alone."

"I love the way you are there for my sisters. You fit right in from the moment I introduced y'all. That's why you are the one I chose to be in my life. I can envision us together for eternity."

Stone turned and smiled at me and I winked at him in return. I felt like shit because our relationship was technically a lie and I wasn't ready to see his reaction when I reveal the truth. Coming to a conclusion in my mind, it wasn't the time to tell Stone anything close to the truth at that point. However, I enjoyed the remainder of the day cuddled in his arms.

Meesha

Chapter 18

Khaos

Phantom called me to fly out to Minnesota with him and I agreed, without giving it a second thought. It was a must for me to join him in this movement because it was time to put a stop to police brutality. Seeing my people killed over and over again was starting to do something to my soul. There had to be something we as people could do to bring this shit to the forefront of the world.

There were many that wanted to act as if it wasn't happening, but it's no longer the sixties. Back then, there wasn't video proof of what was going on, and we have the technology at our fingertips in 2020. The only problem with that is, wasn't shit being done, even with the evidence of what transpired right in our faces. We constantly see our black brothers and sisters dying in real time and the officers don't serve a day behind bars, because the crime committed is always justified. I hoped something different happened though.

Arriving at the airport, the driver stopped the car and attempted to get out. "You don't have to do all that, Marino. I can get the door on my own. Be on standby for when I return," I said, handing him money.

"Thank you, Mr. Scott. I'll be here whenever you call for pickup," Marino said in his Spanish accent.

"Call me Khaos, man. We don't need to do all that formal shit. I'll be sure to hit yo' line when I return."

Exiting the car, I grabbed my bag and made my way across the tarmac, where Phantom was standing in the doorway of the lavish plane. As I made my way up the stairs, my nigga Tim appeared behind Phantom and I knew shit was going to get real from that moment on. When I got to the top of the landing, Phantom had a devilish grin on his face.

"Tim, my nigga! What the fuck you doing in the A?" I asked, giving him a brotherly hug.

"I had to come through and pick up the rest of my team. We're about to fly out to the Twin Cities and fuck some shit up. I know these muthafuckin' cops are about to be on some good bullshit and I'm ready. I hope you came prepared, because it's better to be ready so we won't have to get ready."

"That's what I'm talking about! Hell yeah, I'm locked and loaded," I shot out as I bumped fists with Tim and Phantom.

Making my way down the aisle, I noticed Dreux, Storm, Kane, Killah, and Haze amongst many of Tim's people, seated and buckled in their seats, ready to go. The seat next to Kane was empty and I knew right away that's where I wanted to be. She had a scowl on her face as she typed away on her phone. Sitting next to her, Kane briefly glanced in my direction but went back to what she was doing. I sat in the seat next to her and admired her beauty on the low.

Phantom made his way down the aisle and sat across from us next to Storm. He draped his arm around her shoulders and she automatically shoved him off of her. I chuckled because Storm was too hard for my cousin, and they were going to bump heads every day if they decide to be together in an intimate way. The ongoing battle was going to be about who wore the pants.

"Listen up. When we touch down, keep in mind shit might get ugly. We're going to protest but if it turns into a riot situation, we will be ready. I don't know if any of you have ever dealt with a riot before, but there are many ways for one to get hurt. Staying together is a must! If by chance we are separated," Tim said, holding up earpieces. "We will still be able to stay in touch with one another."

Walking down the aisle, Tim handed each of us one of the devices. As he stood back in the front of the plane, he looked around and smiled. Knowing Tim, he had some shit up his sleeve.

"The pigs will try to beat our asses if things get out of control. Don't back down! We gon' use the same excessive force as them, but we have to let them kick the shit off first. These muthafuckas gon' learn, we are not our ancestors. Slavery's been dead and we want equality around this bitch!" The cheers were deafening in the plane's cabin and everyone was on the same page.

"There are prepacked bookbags for everyone on this plane with room for whatever weapons and ammunition you brought with you.

I'm not gon' lie, I came to shed blood. It's already settled in my mind that some cops gon' die by our hands. Are y'all ready?"

"Hell yeah, fo' sho', no doubt, let's get it," was called out loudly. Tim pulled out his phone and "Fuck tha Police" by NWA blared through the speakers as the plane started rolling towards the runway. Looking over at MaKayla, our eyes locked and she smirked.

"Let's put a wager on who shoots the most police."

"I will never bet my money with you and your sister again. This ain't *Call of Duty*, this is real-life shit, Kayla."

"Kenzie play that video game mess. I shoot live targets. Where ya money at?" she laughed.

"Take yo' ass to sleep before I take you in the bathroom and give you some act-right."

"In your dreams, nigga. We ain't on that. I got enough problems of my own when it comes to a muthafucka, I'm not trying to go there anytime soon."

Kayla turned toward the window as we soared through the sky. All I could think about was how shut off she was about pursuing anything with me. After we return to Atlanta, I was going to finesse the hell out of her in a way money couldn't buy.

Landing at Minneapolis–Saint Paul International Airport, or MSP for short, two and a half hours later, everybody was amped up. We filed off the plane and gathered our bags and got into the awaiting SUV trucks Tim set up for us. There were three total and Tim got in the driver's seat of one, Dreux took over another, and I claimed the last one.

"Follow me, I got us rooms at the Radisson Hotel," Tim said through the earpiece. "I reserved the rooms for two days."

Holding the button while driving, I spoke into the mic. "How much we owe you, fam?"

"We'll deal with that once we get settled in the hotel. For now, we're just gon' concentrate on getting there."

It took about fifteen, twenty minutes to arrive at the hotel. Parking in the lot, we all filed into the lobby and waited patiently for the clerk to give us our keys. We were all assigned two to a room and I was all for it. Of course, Kenzie and Kayla were in a room together and I was with Phantom. Even though I wanted to sleep next to Kayla, in due time that would change for the better.

All the rooms were on the same floor and that was a great set-up. I found the room I would be sleeping in and it was right next to the twins. Dropping my bag on the bed, I sat on one of the queen-sized beds and went straight to my phone to see the latest updates about what was going on. *Twitter* was in an uproar and folks had every right to be. They were demanding the arrest of the officers immediately.

"What you doing, cuz?" Phantom asked, entering the room.

"Checking social media to see what's happening around this muthafucka. I see there's going to be a protest where George lost his life tomorrow."

"We're there. But tonight, I just want to smoke, drink, and chill," Phantom said, digging in his bag.

There was a knock on the adjourning door, and I walked across the room to unlock it. Kenzie walked in with a spiff in her hand with Kayla behind her. Our room turned into the chill spot for the rest of the night, then I passed out on they ass. A nigga was tired as fuck. I'd been up practically all day and needed all my energy for the streets of Minnesota.

***

The next day, I woke up to Phantom cussin'. I rolled over and my eyes landed on the TV screen tuned in on a news station. The reporter was talking about the latest events of the George Floyd case.

"The four officers involved in the death of George Floyd were fired from the police force today. The initial statement that was given by the officers stated Floyd appeared to be under the influence and was resisting arrest. The video that surfaced hours later, told a different story," the reporter announced.

"The mayor of Minneapolis went to social media announcing the termination of the officers, which caused outrage from many all over the country."

Sitting up, I swung my legs from the bed and jumped to my feet. I was pissed because George Floyd lost his life and all they were going to do was fire those muthafuckas! Nah, that's not enough, all four should be charged with murder!

"This the bullshit I'm talking about. Even with video these bitches getting off scot-free. This has been going on long enough and the reason it keeps happening is because police aren't being reprimanded for the shit they do! We gon' have to take this shit back to ninety-two and burn this muthafucka down!"

"I agree, cuz. The only difference is, these cops gon' get charged before it's all said and done." Phantom rolled up and we passed the blunt between us until there was a knock on the door. He got up and let Kenzie in and she stalked past Phantom and sat on the bed.

"Did Heat reach out to either one of y'all?" she asked holding her phone in her hand.

I leaned back and grabbed my phone from the bed and unlocked it. There were two missed calls and a text from Heat that I hadn't heard. When I read the message, I closed it and threw my phone behind me after taking it off silent.

"He called me twice, but my shit was on silent," I said, shrugging my shoulder. "What did he say, Kenzie?" I asked as I turned my body to face her.

"He asked where I was, and I told him none of his business. He started screaming, talking about get to the club now. When I revealed I was out of town, he had the nerve to say I better not be anywhere near Phantom. I just ended the call after that. Heat started calling Kayla's phone and she didn't even answer."

"Well, his ass didn't call me, but I'll be ready whenever he does. What the fuck you do to that nigga, Kenzie?" Phantom laughed. "Heat is wondering like a muthafucka if I'm sampling the pussy he calls his own."

"He can call it what he wants because he will never feel it again. That's the reason you may want to stay in your lane. I would hate for you to start acting up after as you say, sampling the pussy. I'll have to shoot yo' big ass."

Kenzie didn't crack a smile when she said that shit and I knew her ass was missing a few screws. My phone rang and it was Heat. I turned the phone around and showed my cousin who was calling. I answered after letting the phone ring a few times.

"What up, Boss?"

"Look, I've tried calling everybody and nobody is available. I need you to get the team together and get to the club. We have to get back to work since we were backtracked with the shit that happened the other day. Get in touch with Phantom and tell him we got work to do, I'll try the others again."

"Phantom and I won't be available for a couple days, Heat. We had to go out of town to handle some business. I'll hit you up when we touch back down in Atlanta."

"That's the same shit Storm said. Are y'all together?" Heat had the nerve to ask.

"Real talk, that's none of your business," Phantom replied, letting Heat know he could hear him clearly. "We'll be back when we wrap up what we got going on."

"Didn't we have this discussion already? I told you to stay away from her! Where the fuck y'all at?"

Heat was heated and the shit was comical as hell because he was about to bust a blood vessel over a woman he was no longer with. For him to be in his thirties and acting like a jealous teenager, he was making himself look stupid as hell. Kenzie's chest was heaving up and down and I could tell she was trying very hard not to say anything.

"I'm a grown ass man and don't have to abide by your rules. I'm not fuckin' with Kenzie like that no way— yet. We all hung out as a team, but it was on some get to know one another type thing. This shit you doing right now ain't even necessary. We make money together and that's the only thing you should be questioning me about, not a female. That's some hoe shit, homie."

"That's not all the fuck y'all doing! She would never be comfortable enough to tell her first name after just a couple days. Nigga, I know her like the back of my hand!"

"Obviously, you don't know shit about me. What part of mind your business did you get misconstrued? Stop worrying about who I'm doing and put that energy towards Summer's bum ass. Hang up on his ass," Kenzie said, walking back to her room.

"Storm, we need to talk whenever you get back here!" Heat screamed.

"Aye, she ain't in the room no more, man. I'll holla at you later. We should be back tomorrow or Wednesday, but for now, I need to find something to eat." I didn't wait for him to respond before I hung up. Listening to Heat whine like a bitch was something I wasn't with. "I'm hungry as hell, fam. Go tell the girls to get ready so we can go out to eat."

I picked out an outfit and headed to the bathroom while Phantom went to deliver the message to the twins. There was going to be smoke in the city when we got back to Atlanta. Phantom and Heat was going to bump heads hard. I would hate to be Heat when it all comes to a head.

Meesha

Chapter 19

Phantom

The whole team decided to head out together to eat. We were introduced to Tim's people and went over some just in case scenarios as we sat in the restaurant down the street from the hotel. There was a TV playing lowly on the wall. I just so happened to glance up while sipping from my glass of water. A news reporter standing on the street outside the store where George Floyd was killed on East 38th Street and Chicago.

"We gotta go," I said, standing to my feet.

Pointing to the TV, everyone tuned in listening to the reporter as the cameras were directed onto the protesters. I left money on the table and headed for the door. We piled in the trucks and headed back to the hotel to grab our bags before heading to the location. Everyone was in and out within ten minutes and we followed Tim to the location.

"We are going to park several blocks away, then walk over to where the protest is taking place. I don't want us to get blocked in or the vehicles put in a position to get destroyed," Tim said into the earpiece.

"10-4," came through the devices one by one.

We were all in sync with one another and that was a great sign. Tim led us to a public parking lot, and we all lined up next to one another. I looked over at Kenzie and reached over and grabbed her left hand.

"I want you to be careful out there, Kenzie. My eyes will be on you at all times. If I lose sight of you, answer when I reach out over the airwaves. Would you do that for me?"

"Yes, I will stop what I'm doing to let you know I'm okay. But, Phantom, I don't need a babysitter. We got this," she said, getting out of the truck.

Khaos and Kayla had gotten out of the truck moments before, without saying anything. I couldn't just let Kenzie get out without saying be careful. She had to know I cared about her to a certain extent. Walking for several minutes, there were no words spoken.

Up ahead, we saw a slew of people walking with signs and we followed their lead. We made it to the point where the protest was taking place and there were several police standing on the sidewalks with their hands on their guns. They were ready to shoot a muthafucka at any given time. I had my bitch on my hip and I was itching to shoot back, but I had to stay calm even though I was mad at their demeanor as they looked around at the protesters.

Pushing our way through the crowd, I grabbed Kenzie's hand, but she snatched away. I looked over at her and she was grilling the police and her eyes were in slits. Her ass was in full Storm mode and that shit was sexy as hell to me. I was still worried because I didn't know if she would be able to handle herself.

"Go home!" an officer yelled at the crowd through a bullhorn.

"Fuck you, bitch! Fuck twelve!" someone called out.

The phrase was catchy and the entire crowd started chanting, "Fuck twelve." The cops didn't like that shit and they started moving in on the protesters. We hadn't been out there ten minutes before pepper spray was being sprayed into the crowd. Both me and Storm took off our bags and put on the masks Tim provided as part of our kits. It seemed our team were the only group prepared for that shit.

We moved around people that were choking from being sprayed, and Khaos showed up out of nowhere and started walking beside me. There was a Target store down the street, and we headed for it to buy a couple gallons of milk to help the people that were affected by the pepper spray. Taking our masks off, we entered the store and many of the employees were policing the entrance and wouldn't let any of the protesters inside.

"You can't come in here! I don't care what you need, go somewhere else," one of the employees yelled.

"You can't deny us service! We just want to make a muthafuckin' purchase," a young guy screamed back.

"No! We are closed."

"Aight, bet. Let's go y'all. And yo' ass better lock this bitch up too. Get ready for the unemployment line, bitch."

The guy walked away and so did everyone else. Going back onto the street, we went back to chanting with the other protesters. The protesters started moving forward and somebody yelled, "Arrest the cops that killed George Floyd! Charge them with murder! If we don't get it, shut it down!"

Cops didn't like that shit either and a guy standing directly in front of me was shot in the leg and fell to the ground. There was a projectile of what appeared to be a rubber bullet lying next to him. Glancing around, I saw several others that were injured cradling body parts. I frantically looked around and the police were spraying pepper spray once again, but I didn't see anyone with a gun drawn.

A woman fell to the ground and I saw the angle of the rubber bullet hit her right shoulder. Storm was already looking upward, and she sprang to her feet and took off running. I lost sight of her in the crowd and I cussed loudly because she got away from me.

"Storm, get back here!" I screamed into the earpiece. She didn't respond and it pissed me the fuck off. Her ass was a loose cannon and I had a feeling she was about to do something drastic.

"I got her, fam," Tim's voice filled my eardrum. I sighed with relief because she didn't get far.

"Where are you? I'm coming to y'all."

"Nah, everybody head back to the trucks and get ready. The jet will be ready to take off in an hour. Go to the hotel, pack up and wait for me to get there. Trust me."

Tim was out of his mind if he thought I was about to let him do anything without the rest of the team. Especially, not with Storm. He could've asked one of us to get down with him. There was pure pandemonium on the street and Khaos and Kane appeared in front of me.

"What the fuck was that about?" Khaos asked as more people were shot with rubber bullets.

"Storm ran off when someone was shot in front of us. Tim got eyes on her, now they're both on bullshit."

Another shot rang out and Kane howled in pain as she fell to the ground. An officer walked up on us with his weapon drawn and I automatically drew mine. That muthafucka had life fucked up. I looked down at Khaos and Kane and I saw her hand cradling her chest. Kane lifted her shirt and she had on a bulletproof vest that saved her from any injuries. I let out the breath I was holding and pulled the trigger, hitting the cop between the eyes with a real bullet.

"Get up, fam! We gotta shoot our way out of this. These bitches didn't expect for anyone to have weapons to bust back at their asses. Let's see what the fuck their rubber bullets will do now." I pushed the button on the earpiece to talk to the rest of the crew. "I'm in front of the Target, get over here, I just shot a cop!"

Kane jumped up, still rubbing her chest with one hand, while she held a Glock with a silencer in the other. Police were running in our direction and the three of us used them as target practice. Bodies fell like dominoes as we peddled backwards, knocking muthafuckas out of our way.

"Kill all them bitch ass pigs!" somebody screamed, drawing attention to us.

I wanted to send one to his dome because our guns had silencers on them, and his stupid ass wanted to run his mouth. The crowd started scattering in the opposite direction of where we were heading, but then cops were grabbing any and everybody up, beating their asses. The shit wasn't going down in my presence though. I let my bitch sing and the rest of the team followed suit. Police were dropping like flies and the gunfire was coming back at us just as fast. I was ducking and dodging behind any object I could find.

"Fall back! We hit all these muthafuckas, let's go!" I screamed in the earpiece.

I jumped from behind a mailbox and a bullet hit the side of it. Frantically looking around, there weren't any pigs on the ground that were able to bust at us, so I knew there were snipers on one of the roofs above. Trying to pinpoint where the shots were coming from, I peeked above and was almost hit again.

"They got snipers on the roof, stay low, Phantom!" Khaos' voice boomed in my ear.

"Not for long, get ready to haul ass," Storm replied sexily.

Chapter 20

MaKenzie

When the bullet pierced through that woman's arm, I knew them muthafuckas had snipers on the roof of the building on the far side of the street. Phantom called for me to come back, but I wasn't trying to hear none of that shit. My eyes searched back and forth, trying to figure out where the fuck they were hiding. A gleam of light caught my attention and I made a dash for the fire escape that led to the top of the building across from where I spotted the snipers.

I heard Tim say, "I got her, fam," and knew he was on my ass like white on rice. Phantom was trying to come get me himself, but Tim told him he had me. See, I was tired of these cops thinking they would get away with killing our people. So what, they only shot rubber bullets. I'm quite sure the shit didn't feel good and would leave a nice bruise. I had plans to leave many of them cold and stiff.

As I climbed the stairs of the fire escape, my nipples got hard from the thought of getting my own justice for all that lost their lives by the hands of police. I said a silent prayer for the Lord to forgive me before I carried out one of the greatest sins. He had to forgive me for what I was about to do, the same way he forgave the police, politicians, and the President for turning a blind eye to what has been going on with African Americans for years.

It was time for us to demand respect and equality in this fucked-up country. It's a new day and I was ready to set this shit off the right way. Regret was something I wouldn't feel afterwards. If anything, I would feel liberated because playing with the lives of blacks was going to end in 2020.

Getting to the top of the building, I crawled behind the brick chimney and slung the backpack from my back. As I removed the pieces of the TNW Aero Survival rifle I purchased a while ago, I wasted no time putting them in place. Screwing on the silencer, Tim stooped down beside me, and I looked up briefly before snapping the magazine in place.

"What the hell do you think you're doing?"

"They got snipers on the roof! Stay low, Phantom!"

I smirked at Tim and pressed the button. "Not for long. Get ready to haul ass."

The brick wall gave me the perfect position to see the four snipers shooting into the crowd down below. Our team was down there, and the pigs were smiling as they pulled the triggers of their weapons. Tim slung his backpack off and assembled his own weapon as my finger itched to take a shot.

"Don't you dare! I'm not ready! You are outnumbered if they spot you." Tim called himself scolding me.

"Do you hear that? Listen to the people screaming as they are running scared for their lives. Better yet, do you hear what the fuck our team is saying in our ears? Fuck waiting! You better get in where you fit in, because this bitch is about to finish what was started. This is what we geared up for and we will live to tell about it."

Aiming my rifle at the neck of one of the snipers, that was the only part of his body that was exposed. I zoomed in on the scope and pulled the trigger. The blood squirted out like a water hose and I ducked back behind the wall. I could hear the other three snipers cursing and calling out, but I couldn't hear what was being said. Tim stood and stepped out in the open and I followed suit. We shot across to the other building and then there were four snipers dead on the rooftop.

"Let's go. You a bad muthafucka and I like the way you move. You're deadly and I wouldn't want to be on your bad side. When we get back on the ground, we have to go another route."

"Nah, we're going through the building. They probably got the chance to summon their colleagues. We have to disappear," I said, rushing to the metal door on the other side.

The door was locked and I shot that muthafucka until the bolt gave way. Me and Tim ran down thirteen flights of stairs. Yeah, I was counting. When we made it to the ground floor, Tim took the lead and peeked out of the door. We made our exit with guns in hand. The building was some type of office space and the lobby was empty. Tim tried the door and it was locked, but that didn't stop anything on our end.

There were people still running wild in the streets and it had turned into a full-blown riot outside the building. Tim shot the lock and it gave way. Stepping out on the street, I raised my hand to communicate with the team, but Phantom beat me to the punch.

"Where the fuck is y'all? Storm, answer me!"

"We heading to the whips. What's your location?" Tim asked.

"We waiting on y'all. We kicked that shit off, nigga!" Phantom yelled. "Get here so we can bail out."

"They're burning this muthafucka up! Give us a few to get to y'all. I'm about to hit up the pilot to let him know were on the way."

I walked backwards slowly as Tim kept his eye on what was going on in front of us. The scene before me was one for the books, because my people were showing these muthafuckas playtime was over. There were a couple EMTs helping the wounded and sheets were covering the officers we popped. The attention wasn't on us, even though we had weapons out in the open making our getaway.

"You handled yourself back there, sista. I want you to take this advice from me today," Tim said as we entered the parking lot. "What you're doing is good and you do it well. I want you to think before you react. You mean well in how you handle yourself and the ones around you but, being smart about your moves is just as important."

Nodding my head, I knew I could be a hothead at times and for someone that didn't know anything about me to speak on it, made me open my ears to soak everything he said in. As we got closer to the trucks, Phantom jumped out and stomped in my direction. I held my hand up and attempted to walk around him.

"Don't walk away from me!"

"I know what I did was wrong, Phantom." I snatched away and turned to face him. "But I had to make a move to get them pigs off the roof. We don't have time for this shit right now, we're hot and need to get to the plane."

Opening the door to the truck I saw Phantom get out of, Kayla ran over and threw her arms around my neck. There were no words exchanged, but I knew my sister was glad to see me alive and well. She went back to the truck behind me and I got in and sat, waiting for us to pull off. My head fell back onto the headrest and I closed my eyes as I thought back to what I'd done.

"You alright?" Phantom asked as he climbed into the backseat next to me.

"Yeah. I don't want to talk about it."

Turning toward the window, I watched as one of Tim's guys drove us away from Minneapolis and straight to the airport.

***

There was a lot of talk about what happened on the plane, but I didn't feel like reliving that shit. Placing my air pods in my ears, I drifted off to sleep until we landed back in Atlanta. The only thing I wanted to do was go home, take a shower and go to bed. Standing from my seat, I waited patiently for Phantom to do the same, so I could get my bag and make my exit.

"Sit down, Kenzie," he said, without looking at me.

"I'm ready to get off this plane, Phantom. I'm tired."

He ignored me by continuing to scroll through his phone. Counting backwards from ten, I took a deep breath and closed my eyes. When I opened them again, Phantom was staring at me with a firm expression on his face.

"Whatever you're thinking about doing, I'd advise you not to do it. We will get off shortly, just relax."

Phantom finally got up and retrieved both of our bags and led the way to the front of the plane. I stepped off the last step and followed him to a black SUV. Kayla and Khaos was already seated inside in the far back. I knew Phantom was mad at me, but he hadn't attempted to talk to me since earlier when we were back in Minnesota.

It was almost ten o'clock and the sky was riddled with stars, and the light breeze was brushing against my skin. I couldn't wait to get home, but I would have to talk things out with Phantom before I could even think about getting any type of rest. The driver pulled up in front of Phantom's house and he got out to get his bag from the trunk.

"Why are you still sitting there, Kenzie? This is our stop."

"I'm going home. I don't know what made you think I was staying here with you," I retorted.

"Let me rephrase what I said. Get out of the truck, Kenzie. We need to talk." Phantom walked off and I had no choice but to get out because he had my bag that held my keys in it.

"Sis, go talk to him. If you need me to come back to pick you up, I will," Kayla said, getting out of the truck to hug me. "You did good out there, Kenzie. I don't see anything wrong with what happened today. You moved and we reacted in the correct manner. I think Phantom just wants to make sure you're okay."

"I'll talk to him, but he better keep that shit funky without aggression, because I'm not for the bullshit. When I'm ready, I'll hit your line. I love you, sis."

Stepping back from my sister, I watched as she got back inside the truck and waited until they drove away before I made my way towards Phantom's home. The door was left slightly open so I could enter the premises. I closed the door and locked it and made my way inside to find Phantom. Passing the living room, it was empty. The same for the kitchen as well. I decided to just call out, because I didn't know the layout of his home.

"Phantom!" I called out as I walked slowly.

"I'm on the patio. Come on out, Kenzie."

Following Phantom's voice, I stepped out of the house and he was sitting shirtless, smoking a blunt. He nodded towards my purse and I immediately grabbed it to roll up myself. Both of us were quiet as I touched the tip of the wood with fire from my lighter. The smoke filled my lungs and I relaxed instantly.

"Kenzie, what were you thinking, running off like you did in Minnesota?" Phantom finally asked after being quiet while I got settled.

"I wasn't thinking, reacting was what I did. Those muthafuckin pigs were shooting into the crowd like we were fuckin' animals! It was either I stood with y'all or get rid of the problem that was hiding high up. I chose the latter, because I knew y'all would be able to handle what was happening on the ground."

"That is not the point, Kenzie. I saw what they were doing, I was right there. Anything could've happened to you when you ran off. Shit, they could've shot you in the fuckin' back or something," Phantom said, sitting up as he glared at me.

"That didn't happen so let's not think about the woulda, coulda, shoulda's. We got out of the situation and that should be what matters at this point. When we agreed to go to Minnesota, we all knew what the hell we were going to do before we arrived. We handled that shit, Phantom. Now we just have to make sure the shit don't come back to bite us in the ass. As for now, we killed a slew of cops the way they have done hundreds of blacks and got away with the shit."

"Don't ever do that shit again, man. I understand you're used to working how you want and when you want, but it's not just you and Kayla anymore. There's a strong team standing ten toes down with y'all now. Include me in your decisions. It's not a secret that I give a fuck about you, but I'm here to let you know."

I puffed hard on the blunt because Phantom was putting his feelings on display and I wasn't feeling it at all. My heart was not made for loving another in the way he hoped. I had Heat to thank for the way my heart was set up. The last thing I wanted to do was hurt Phantom's feelings, because he thought there would be more between us other than friendship.

"Well, don't give a fuck about me, Phantom. Like I told you before, the feelings are not mutual." Shifting in my seat, I stared him square in the eyes and said, "I'm attracted to you and would have no problem sleeping with you. The problems will definitely come into play when I fuck you and still treat you like one of the homies. Would you be able to handle that?"

Phantom snubbed out his blunt and stood to his feet. Rounding the table, he took my wood from my hand and put it out. "Let's find out," he said, gathering me in his arms and carried me in the house.

"Phantom, put me down!" I shrieked, trying to wiggle out of his grip.

"Shut the fuck up, Kenzie," he growled, biting the side of my neck. "I'm about to show you I'm not trying to hear shit you talking about. I'm willing to be your friend with benefits, but that shit won't last too long with the dick I'm about to deliver to yo' ass."

Phantom moved rapidly up the stairs after locking the patio door and I was already tired and had no more fight in me. I couldn't pry myself out of his muscular arms for anything in the world. His hand entered the back of my leggings and I turned to putty as my love box turned on me by soaking his fingers when he pushed two inside slowly. The low moan that fell from my lips made his man bounce in the basketball shorts he wore.

We entered his bedroom and the coolness of his central air caressed my ass crack. Phantom placed me gently on the bed and the thought of making a run for it was short-lived when he yanked my pants down in one swoop. My flip-flops were tangled in the legs of the pants and thrown behind the man that stood before me. Phantom pried my legs apart and dropped to his knees.

"Nope, nope, nope," I said, breathing heavily while pushing at his head.

The nigga had a strong ass neck, so that alone told me he was about to put in work on my clit, if I didn't get him away from me. I couldn't allow that. The more I pushed, the harder he pressed forward. Phantom grabbed my thighs and scooted my ass off the bed and pinned my legs upward until my feet were touching my ears. His tongue slid along my slit and I shivered from head to toe.

"Oh, my God! We can't do this, Phantom," I moaned as my toes threw up all types of gang signs.

He tuned out my cries and continued what he started. With one hand, he held both of my legs and I stopped fighting instantly when his lips wrapped around my love bud. The tingling sensation I felt in my stomach was intense and I knew I was about to explode in his mouth. My legs went rigid and I moaned out sexily, "Yes! Fuck!"

Phantom never came up for air as he kept devouring my pussy like it was his last supper. His fingers parted my lower lips and he licked up all of my juices as that tingle returned. I bucked against his mouth and there wasn't an ounce of fight left in me. I welcomed the feeling he gave me and was loving every bit of it. Reaching around my legs, I grabbed the back of his head while grinding my hips to the tune that played in my mind.

"Shit, right there! Just like that, Phantom. Aaaah!"

I felt his finger enter my forbidden hole and the shit felt so good, it made me buck harder and another orgasm was building. There was nothing I could do but let that shit ride. The wave that man was taking me on was one I'd never surfed ever in life. I didn't want to come down from the spell he had me under. As he sucked hard on my clit, I squirted all over his face and my body went limp.

"Yeah, talk that shit now," he said, rising to his full height as he snatched his shorts down, revealing his long python.

My eyes followed his every move as he went to the nightstand next to the bed and retrieved a Magnum XL condom. I didn't have the strength to move, but in all honesty, I wanted to fuck him just as much as he wanted to fuck me. Two years was a long time for any woman to go without having relations. I needed him to knock the Mario coins out of my pussy and he better come through too.

"Get yo' ass on all fours and arch that back!"

I did what he demanded, and the shit was sexy as fuck to me. I loved a man that took charge with what he wanted. Talking shit was my forte and I loved a man that talked that shit right along with me. When I was in position, Phantom eased behind me and rubbed his dick up and down my slit before placing his tip at my opening.

"Damn, Kenzie! You tight than a muthafucka," he growled. "Yeah, this shit is about to be better than it tasted."

Moving in and out of me slowly, the anticipation of him getting all the way in was on an all-time high. I couldn't wait for him to pacify my pussy, I pushed back and continued to bounce until I felt him in my guts. Grabbing a fistful of the sheet on his bed, I bounced back hard.

"Yes! Fuck the shit outta me, Phantom," I screamed out in ecstasy.

"Oh, now you want this shit, huh? I'm not ready to give you all this dick just yet," he laughed. "You gon' wait until I want you to have all I can provide. With yo' hardheaded ass."

My eyes expanded because he said he wasn't giving it all to me, but hell, it felt like he had at least nine inches inside of my shit already. Phantom grabbed a handful of my ass and kissed down my spine before plunging inside of my wetness. My breath caught and I felt something pop in my lady parts. I knew damn well this nigga couldn't have popped my cherry. I was far from a virgin.

"Fuck! Yo' pussy is so good, girl. I'm about to mold this muthafucka to fit my dick and my dick only. You done fucked up, Kenzie. This my shit now, baby."

We sexed each other for hours without taking any breaks. It was a good thing I was still on the pill, even though I wasn't having sex with anyone. I didn't know when I was going to have a hot girl moment and kids weren't on my agenda at all.

Phantom sucked every crevice of my body, but not once did I reciprocate the favor. The nigga was going crazy from my sugary walls, I didn't need him catching a case because of my head game, that shit was lethal. He would have to be my man in order for that to happen, but that's not what I was on. I felt giving in to him was going to be a huge problem waiting to happen. We both fell asleep as the sun shined through the blinds, with smiles on our faces.

Meesha

Chapter 21

Heat

The things that were going on in the world was fucked up, but my mind was on Kenzie and Phantom's muthafuckin' ass. I guess they thought I was a joke. When I told her to stay the fuck away from him, she didn't listen and neither did he. Showing both of them I meant business was what I would have to do. And I knew exactly how I was going to pierce Kenzie's heart.

I was lying in bed and the last thing I should've been doing was thinking about MaKenzie Jones. Summer was snoring quietly beside me and I felt bad because I wished she was Kenzie. Getting up, I grabbed my phone and the time read one in the morning. I needed to put my plan into play immediately. Walking slowly down the stairs, I found Big Will's name in my contacts and hit the button.

"Hey, Will. Sorry to call so late. I need you and Rocko to head out to Houston tomorrow," I spoke into the phone soon as Big Will answered.

"Heat, have you been watching what the fuck is going on? Muthafuckas are mad because of what happened to dude in Minnesota."

"What do that have to do with you and Rocko going to Houston? Not a damn thing! You know I sent Tornado to get with that nigga Stone and her ass ain't did shit in almost a year. It's up to you and Rocko to go handle that situation and while y'all at it, handle that bitch too!" Taking a seat on the sofa in the living room, I pulled my weed box from the drawer of the table and proceeded to roll up.

Big Will was quiet for a minute before he let out a deep breath. "Look, Heat. I helped train those girls to be better than they were when they came to work for you."

"And?"

"They are like my family, man. I'm not about to kill her. Don't make me do that, Heat."

This was the shit that pissed me off. The twins won everybody over when they came onboard with the team, but I wasn't letting anyone save those bitches or their feelings, this time around. It didn't matter the reason I was doing what I planned, the shit just needed to be done. Big Will didn't want to go against me. At least, he wouldn't if he wanted to continue living a good life.

"I'm not trying to hear none of that, fam. It's us against the world, remember? I need you to go scope out that nigga's every move until I tell you when to take action. Find out why Tornado hasn't completed the job. I'm not asking you, Will. I'm now telling you. I'll call Rocko and fill him in. You already know not to talk about this to any other member of the team, especially Storm."

"What the fuck is going on with you and Storm, Heat? Shit been crazy with y'all since she returned. It ain't never been that way with the two of y'all."

"She thinks I don't know she's fuckin' with that nigga Phantom—"

"Wait, yo' ass in yo' feelings because of who she's dealing with? She's young and is entitled to explore life. Plus, you have Summer. Concentrate on her, man."

"Do I look like I need yo' muthafuckin' ass to philosophize to me? I didn't ask for yo' opinion on what the fuck I'm doing over here. Stay out my business and concentrate on the job I just laid in yo' lap. I'll handle Storm. All I want you to do is get to Houston."

I hung up on his ass and put fire to the blunt I'd rolled while on the phone. Inhaling deeply, my thoughts were all on Storm. I picked my phone up to give her a call, but I heard a noise to my left. Summer was leaned against the wall with a scowl on her face. I didn't know how much of my conversation she'd heard, but that was on her because she had no business eavesdropping on my conversation. That's what the fuck she got for ear hustling.

"Why are you standing there like a bump on a fuckin' log, Summer?" I asked irritably, pulling on the blunt.

"Why the fuck you have to leave the room to talk about that bitch?" I hated when she answered a question with a question. That shit irked my damn nerves. All she had to do was respond to what the hell I asked her.

Savage Storms

"This my fuckin' house! I can do whatever I want in this mutha-fucka. If you weren't listening so hard, you would've known what was said. It was business," I shot back.

"So, who she's fuckin' is business? Get the fuck outta here with that bullshit, Romero! If you want the bitch, go be with her! I'm tired of this bullshit. You've been up my ass since she vanished and now that she's back, you talk to me like I ain't shit. On top of that, your attitude is different, you fuck me differently, and you treat me as a bitch of convenience. Why is that?"

Summer walked further into the room with her arms folded over her chest. The hurt in her eyes made a nigga feel bad, because eve-rything she said was true. I didn't do it purposely, but I told her time and time again if she didn't agree with not being in a relationship exclusively, to leave me alone. She was the one that decided to ride it out. Now, she wanted to stand up to me and talk as if I was cheat-ing on her.

"You notice that type of shit because in your mind, I'm your man, Summer. That's your reality, not mine. I've explained how this was gon' be from the beginning. You're the one that changed the dynamics of what we got on yo' end. I'm still moving the same way I've been from jump. Get out ya feelings, because you have no right to be mad every time a bitch name comes outta my mouth."

I already knew how Summer was about to react because it was the same, each time I had to remind her of not being my woman. It was about to be different though because I didn't have time for her bullshit. She knew exactly what she was signing up for when she continued to slob on my nut sack.

"One thing you won't have the freedom to do is dictate who I entertain. I'm gon' tell you for the last time, Summer, if you can't handle the heat, get the fuck out the kitchen. I went wrong when I started wining and dining yo' ass by giving you things, letting you sleepover at my crib, and showed yo' ass affection. Hurting you was never in my plans, but I thought you understood where we stood. Now, I have to put an end to all of this shit because the last thing I need in my life is drama. I'd rather walk away than deal with un-necessary bullshit."

171

"You know what, you're right. I'm not your woman but you treated me as such. I guess everything you showed me didn't mean nothing to you because it was something for you to do while your precious Kenzie was away. I get it, Heat. I'm just a filler for the one you really want in your life. You don't have to worry about me anymore, I'm done."

Summer turned to walk away, and I stood from the sofa following her up the stairs. I could be an asshole at times, but I didn't want to allow her to leave at that time of the morning. If anything, I wanted us to remain friends without any animosity between us. I had to play this shit right because Summer was the manager of my establishment and she was damn good at her job. Jeopardizing our work relationship was what I didn't want to happen.

"Look, Summer. It's not that I don't care for you. I can't give you what you're looking for as far as a relationship, but our friendship is very important to me. We won't be able to establish a relationship together if both parties aren't ready."

"Nah, Heat, get it right. You're not ready to be in a relationship, but you're quick to act like I belong to you when a nigga in my face at the club. You want to be the only nigga *I'm* fuckin', but you're out there passing out dick like candy. I'm over allowing you to decide when you want to be with me, and I don't have the same options."

"That's the problem. You ain't me," I laughed, causing her scowl to deepen. "Stop trying to do shit because you believe it's going to piss me off. I already know what it is between us, you need to follow suit. We fuck, go out, and enjoy one another's company. I don't want a title and you do, so we are far from the same. Stay in your place, Summer. That's the reason yo' ass on the verge of tears now. You let your feelings lead you to a dead-end and the fault is yours."

The tears Summer was trying hard to hold back, slid down her cheeks rapidly. I didn't feel any remorse because I told her what it was, and she said she understood the stipulations. She went after me, thinking she would get the same treatment I gave Kenzie and that wasn't the case. Slowly slipping on her clothes, Summer walked around my bedroom collecting her belongings.

"I'm not going to let you leave at this time of the night, Summer. Stay in here and get some sleep, I'll sleep in the guest bedroom. If you still feel you want to leave at daybreak, have at it. But I don't want you driving around out there this late with everything that's happening right now."

Summer sat on the bed and bawled loudly. I didn't want to console her, because it would make her think I gave a fuck in a way other than me caring about her wellbeing. Instead, I walked to the dresser and posted up with my arms crossed over my chest, waiting for her to cry it out so I could go back to sleep. Summer always tried to emotionalize her way into my heart, and it worked for the most part, but I wasn't having it at that moment.

"Look, lay down and get some sleep. We can talk more about it later if that's what you want to do."

"I won't be here later, Heat. I'll stay until the sun comes up, then I'm going home. From this point on, don't say shit about anything I do when you see me out and about. I've done nothing but showed you the utmost respect for the past two years and you never gave a fuck about me. You want to act like there was never anything between us, I'll let you have that. Watch me do me, like you've been doing the entire duration of our situationship. Close the door behind you on your way out."

Summer eased out of her clothes and my dick bricked up. Pushing off the dresser, I glanced at her voluptuous ass and forced myself to leave the room without approaching her. In my mind I wanted to smash, but I knew it would send mixed signals and opted to do without the pussy. Summer was going to entice me to fuck again one day and if I wanted it sooner, I'm confident I would be able to ease between her cheeks.

Entering the guest bedroom, I closed and locked the door, then crawled between the sheets. I sent Rocko a text letting him know what I expected from him and Big Will, before I laid down and passed out.

Meesha

Chapter 22

Nicassy

It's been a couple weeks since I'd talked to Scony, but I still hadn't sat down to talk to Stone. To be honest, I was nervous as hell because nothing good could come out of telling a man you have fallen in love with, you were originally supposed to kill him. Chewing on my bottom lip while wiping down nonexistent dust around the room, I glanced around at all of the nice things Stone had bought me over time.

None of that shit mattered to me, because I had a nice nest egg of my own and I didn't need him to do anything for me monetarily. I was tired of pretending we met by chance and wanted to be honest with Stone about everything. How I was going to start the conversation, was the problem I was having. Stone went out earlier while I was sleeping and I had no idea when he would return.

Deciding to take a long hot shower and wash my hair, I grabbed a pair of leggings, my Queen Hustle shirt by Meesha and walked into the bathroom. Looking at myself in the mirror, I had bags under my eyes along with dark circles. Sleep was hard to come by when I had so much going on in my head. Stone's perspective of me was bound to change after I revealed the truth to him. I removed the nightshirt I was wearing and turned the shower on, making the water hot as hell.

As I stepped inside, a lone tear rolled down my cheek because I knew my life with Stone was going to be over after that day. Reminiscing about all the good times we had put a slight smile on my face. But the thought of the man I've come to love not even knowing my real name, tugged at my heart. The deception I displayed was the worse a woman could ever do to a man. On top of that, my life would be in jeopardy because he might kill me before hearing why I didn't follow through with Heat's plan.

After lathering my hair with shampoo, I rinsed and washed my body a few times before stepping out of the shower. Wrapping a towel around my wet hair, I did the same with my body as I stood in front of the mirror to comb out my long tresses. Applying moisturizer to my hair, I wrapped it up and put a scarf on to hold it in place.

"You look so tired, baby," Stone spoke softly behind me. "Is everything alright?" I lowered my head slightly but snapped it back upright quickly. Turning to face him, I opened my mouth to speak and the tears started rolling from my eyes. "Angel, what's wrong?" he asked, gathering me in his arms.

"We need to talk," I forced out between sobs.

"What could you possibly have to talk about that has you in such a mess?" Stone asked, leading me into the bedroom. I sat on the bed and he rubbed my back as I cried quietly. "Talk to me, Angel. You haven't been yourself lately and I don't like what I've been witnessing."

Easing out of his grasp, I scooted over on the bed and tucked my right leg under my left thigh. Clearing my throat, I fidgeted with my hands and chewed on my lip vigorously. Stone reached over and pried it from my teeth gently and kissed me on the corner of my mouth. I caressed his beard and placed my forehead against his and closed my eyes.

"Stone, I have to be honest with you. My name is not Angel. That's what my granny called me when I was younger. My real name is Nicassy Avers," I said, sighing heavily.

"Okay. That's nothing to cry about, love."

"There's more," I paused. "The night I met you at Club Onyx, it wasn't by coincidence. I was sent to kill you." My voice quivered and I couldn't stop the tears from flowing.

Stone was quiet for a while but when I opened my mouth to continue, he raised his hand and silenced me. The concerned expression he possessed turned into one of anger. Standing to his feet, Stone moved across the room to put space between us.

"Stone, I'm sorry—"

"Shut the fuck up, Angel, or whatever your name is! You've been living in my house and had me under the impression that you were all for me! I've been sleeping comfortably while yo' stankin' ass been sitting back plottin' on how to kill my stupid ass! This is the reason I hadn't gotten into any serious relationships, and I should've smashed and passed on yo' ass too!"

"Baby, I swear I have not plotted on you at all. Once I got to know you as a person, killing you was the furthest thing from my mind. I've grown to love you—"

"Love me? How the fuck is that possible when you sought me out to murk my ass? Who the fuck sent you, bitch?"

"Stone, would you please let me explain without cutting me off?" I asked, pushing off the bed.

Stone's arm went behind his back and the barrel of a gun was pointed at my head. "Sit the fuck down before I fill yo' ass with some hot shit! Fuck all that other shit, who sent you to come for me?"

At that moment, I knew I had start talking and fast. The scene was playing out just as I feared, and I was ready to piss on myself. I was scared as hell and there was really nothing that I could do to save my life, other than tell the truth. The look in Stone's eyes were one I had never seen before and I was terrified.

"Heat! I work as a hit woman for a guy named Romero "Heat" Ramirez. He sent me here to kill you because he said you were a pedophile and liked to mess around with young girls. I took the job because I hate a man that likes to fondle kids. I'm sorry, Stone. I really am and I've learned over time, you aren't the man Heat perceived you to be."

Stone slightly lowered his weapon as he looked at me quizzingly. "Heat sent you to kill me?" he laughed. "I'm the muthafucka that gives him the jobs to send his team on! That nigga on some fuck shit and sent a female to do his dirty work. I understand where this is coming from now. Get yo' shit and get out of my muthafuckin' house, bitch! I don't deal with sneaky muthafuckas of any kind. Usually, you would be dead by now, swimming in a pool of water waiting to be discovered. By the time I come back, I want you and all yo' shit outta my crib."

Stone stuck his gun back in the small of his back and left the room, pulling his shirt down to hide it. As bad as I wanted to run behind him, I knew not to because I had another chance at life. He could've shot me without blinking and I would've deserved every bullet that entered my body. Instead, I walked to the closet and grabbed my luggage to start packing for my trip to Atlanta.

"One more thing," Stone said, appearing in the doorway. "Don't take shit outta here my money bought. Take whatever you came in this bitch with. Call your boss and let him know he fucked up comin' for me," he said, leaving back out.

The door slammed as he made his exit and all I could do was cry as I packed. I truly believed Stone was my happily ever after, but I would never know for sure because deception didn't get you very far in life.

Chapter 23

Stone

When I heard Angel tell me why she entered my life, I wanted to kill her ass on sight. I fell in love with her just as she fell for me, but I couldn't overlook the fact that our entire relationship was based on a lie. Now, that muthafuckin' Heat, that nigga was going to get what was coming to his ass. He ate off the strength of me and sent somebody to eliminate me, over what? I didn't know, but I had plans to find out.

I jumped in my ride with no destination in mind, but I knew I had to give Angel the time needed to get her shit and get out of my crib. A nigga was lowkey hurt because I had plans to make the bitch my wife one day. She got along with my family, we laughed together, and I let her in on every aspect of my life. I regretted that shit because I didn't even know her real fuckin' name until that day. I had to talk to somebody about this shit because my mind was on going back to the house to snuff her ass out.

I leaned to the side as I retrieved my phone from my back pocket. Going through my contacts, I found my homie's name and pressed on it to call him up. As I pulled to a red light, he answered after a few rings and it was good that he did. My mind was telling me to turn around to make that bitch disappear.

"Long time no hear, fam. What's good with ya?"

"Man, Scony," I said, shaking my head as I pulled off from the light soon as it turned green. "I've been fuckin' with this broad for several months and I want to kill this hoe."

"What? You got an exclusive bitch? Not Stone," he laughed.

Scony and I had been doing business together for a couple of years since he got out of the drug game. I ran a business idea by him, and he went in with me and we split the profits fifty-fifty, but I run it until I need him to come in to help. I've had everything under control the whole while through, but I needed my homie to talk me down from what I really wanted to do.

"Yeah, unfortunately I let my guard down and this bitch got in my head like no other has ever been able to do. Let me tell you what this muthafucka had the nerve to tell me, fam. I started fuckin' with this nigga named Heat a couple years ago. I put him on when I opened the business and we were cool. I don't know what the fuck he got against me, but he put a hit out on a nigga and sends this bitch to carry out the job."

"Wait, Heat? Where is this muthafucka from?" Scony asked, cutting in before I could continue.

"He's from Atlanta. The nigga has a club there called Club Heat and he has a team that does jobs I send to him. Anyway, this bitch been lovey-dovey with me for damn near a year and wanted to cleanse her conscience and tell me the muthafucka sent her to kill me. She claims she loves me, but I'm not buying that shit. Even though she had ample chances to murk me but didn't. She claimed she loved me, but how? The bitch was looking at hundreds of thousands to complete the mission."

"Hold up, Stone. Please tell me you didn't kill her." The hurt in my man's voice was evident when he spoke.

"Nah, I told the bitch to have her shit packed and to be gone by the time I got back to the crib. I pulled my tool, but my heart wouldn't allow me to pull the trigga. Angel was everything I've ever wanted in a woman and the bitch was a snake the whole time. I swear, I wanted to bust her shit open like a fuckin' watermelon, but I couldn't do it."

Scony breathed a sigh of relief. "I'm glad you didn't. Angel, I mean, Nicassy is like a sister to me. She called me a couple weeks ago and told me about the job Heat sent her on. My biological sisters work for him too and they don't know shit about the assignment Heat sent Nicassy on. If she said she loves you, Stone, she meant that shit. If she wanted to kill you, believe me, you wouldn't be having this conversation with me if it was about money. I trained those girls myself. I don't agree with the direction they chose to live their lives, but I respect it."

"Hold up! You know Angel?" I asked, stunned.

180

"Yes, and I'm sorry you had to find out the way you did. She mentioned the name Stone, but I didn't think it was you. I told her to get the fuck away from you, but I see she didn't listen. Nicassy tries to make shit right when she's in the wrong, for the most part anyway. It's been a long time coming, for her to find a man she could develop something with, she just went about that shit wrong. I don't blame you for telling her to leave, I would've killed her ass, to be honest."

"I couldn't bring myself to do it. I love her, man. Being with her is something I can't see myself doing after this. Hopefully, she's gone when I get back home. It was good while it lasted. I can promise she'll be alive and well the next time you reach out to her," I said, cutting the car off after parking in front of the restaurant to get some wings. "Let me go in here and order my food. I'll hit you up a little later, fam. Thanks for hearing me out, but that nigga Heat got some explaining to do."

"Keep me posted on when you gon' ride down on his ass. I want to be front and center because he put my family in danger. I'm gon' call my sister and fill her in on what's going on too. Stay up my nigga, I got yo' back whenever you need me."

Ending the call, I had many mixed emotions after talking to Scony. The world was small as fuck, but I couldn't go back on what I said to Angel even if I wanted to. It was best for us to go our separate ways. I got out of my brand-new 2020 Porsche Panamera and went inside the restaurant to order a platter of wings. My mind kept going back to Angel, but I shook that shit off, but the feeling that something wasn't right was strong.

When my number was called, I snatched the bag and rushed to my whip and peeled out of the parking lot. I drove above the speed limit but not too much to draw attention of the pigs that were always lurking in the cut, waiting to pull my black ass over for driving a car worth more money than they made in a year. As I neared my home, the butterflies in my stomach were going wild. I couldn't shake the feeling and I didn't like that shit.

I pulled into the driveway and cut the engine. Grabbing the bag of wings, I got out and headed up the walkway. Inserting my key, I twisted the doorknob and opened the door. A loud explosion ignited soon as I attempted to step forward. I was blown back out of the door and all I could think was, did Angel get out. Trying to lift my head, I couldn't as darkness took over and my body went limp.

To Be Continued...
Savage Storms 2
Coming Soon

Submission Guideline

Submit the first three chapters of your completed manuscript to ldpsubmissions@gmail.com, subject line: Your book's title. The manuscript must be in a .doc file and sent as an attachment. Document should be in Times New Roman, double spaced and in size 12 font. Also, provide your synopsis and full contact information. If sending multiple submissions, they must each be in a separate email.

Have a story but no way to send it electronically? You can still submit to LDP/Ca$h Presents. Send in the first three chapters, written or typed, of your completed manuscript to:

LDP: Submissions Dept
Po Box 944
Stockbridge, Ga 30281

DO NOT send original manuscript. Must be a duplicate.

Provide your synopsis and a cover letter containing your full contact information.

Thanks for considering LDP and Ca$h Presents.

Coming Soon from Lock Down Publications/Ca$h Presents

BOW DOWN TO MY GANGSTA

By **Ca$h**

TORN BETWEEN TWO

By **Coffee**

THE STREETS STAINED MY SOUL **II**

By **Marcellus Allen**

BLOOD OF A BOSS **VI**

SHADOWS OF THE GAME II

By **Askari**

LOYAL TO THE GAME **IV**

By **T.J. & Jelissa**

A DOPEBOY'S PRAYER **II**

By **Eddie "Wolf" Lee**

IF LOVING YOU IS WRONG... **III**

By **Jelissa**

TRUE SAVAGE **VII**

MIDNIGHT CARTEL III

DOPE BOY MAGIC IV

CITY OF KINGZ II

By **Chris Green**

BLAST FOR ME **III**

A SAVAGE DOPEBOY III

CUTTHROAT MAFIA II

By **Ghost**

A HUSTLER'S DECEIT III

KILL ZONE **II**

BAE BELONGS TO ME III

A DOPE BOY'S QUEEN II

Savage Storms

By **Aryanna**
COKE KINGS V
KING OF THE TRAP II
By **T.J. Edwards**
GORILLAZ IN THE BAY V
De'Kari
THE STREETS ARE CALLING II
Duquie Wilson
KINGPIN KILLAZ IV
STREET KINGS III
PAID IN BLOOD III
CARTEL KILLAZ IV
DOPE GODS II
Hood Rich
SINS OF A HUSTLA II
ASAD
KINGZ OF THE GAME V
Playa Ray
SLAUGHTER GANG IV
RUTHLESS HEART IV
By **Willie Slaughter**
THE HEART OF A SAVAGE III
By **Jibril Williams**
FUK SHYT II
By **Blakk Diamond**
FEAR MY GANGSTA 5
THE REALEST KILLAZ II
By **Tranay Adams**
TRAP GOD II
By **Troublesome**

Meesha

YAYO IV
A SHOOTER'S AMBITION III
By S. Allen
GHOST MOB
Stilloan Robinson
KINGPIN DREAMS III
By Paper Boi Rari
CREAM
By Yolanda Moore
SON OF A DOPE FIEND II
By Renta
FOREVER GANGSTA II
GLOCKS ON SATIN SHEETS III
By Adrian Dulan
LOYALTY AIN'T PROMISED II
By Keith Williams
THE PRICE YOU PAY FOR LOVE II
DOPE GIRL MAGIC III
By Destiny Skai
CONFESSIONS OF A GANGSTA II
By Nicholas Lock
I'M NOTHING WITHOUT HIS LOVE II
By Monet Dragun
CAUGHT UP IN THE LIFE III
By Robert Baptiste
LIFE OF A SAVAGE IV
A GANGSTA'S QUR'AN II
By **Romell Tukes**
QUIET MONEY III
THUG LIFE II

By **Trai'Quan**
THE STREETS MADE ME III
By **Larry D. Wright**
THE ULTIMATE SACRIFICE VI
IF YOU CROSS ME ONCE II
ANGEL III
By **Anthony Fields**
THE LIFE OF A HOOD STAR
By Ca$h & Rashia Wilson
FRIEND OR FOE II
By **Mimi**
SAVAGE STORMS II
By **Meesha**

Available Now

RESTRAINING ORDER **I & II**
By **CA$H & Coffee**
LOVE KNOWS NO BOUNDARIES **I II & III**
By **Coffee**
RAISED AS A GOON I, II, III & IV
BRED BY THE SLUMS I, II, III
BLAST FOR ME I & II
ROTTEN TO THE CORE I II III
A BRONX TALE I, II, III
DUFFEL BAG CARTEL I II III IV
HEARTLESS GOON I II III IV

A SAVAGE DOPEBOY I II

HEARTLESS GOON I II III

DRUG LORDS I II III

CUTTHROAT MAFIA

By **Ghost**

LAY IT DOWN **I & II**

LAST OF A DYING BREED

BLOOD STAINS OF A SHOTTA I & II III

By **Jamaica**

LOYAL TO THE GAME I II III

LIFE OF SIN I, II III

By **TJ & Jelissa**

BLOODY COMMAS I & II

SKI MASK CARTEL I II & III

KING OF NEW YORK I II,III IV V

RISE TO POWER I II III

COKE KINGS I II III IV

BORN HEARTLESS I II III IV

KING OF THE TRAP

By **T.J. Edwards**

IF LOVING HIM IS WRONG…I & II

LOVE ME EVEN WHEN IT HURTS I II III

By **Jelissa**

WHEN THE STREETS CLAP BACK I & II III

THE HEART OF A SAVAGE I II

By **Jibril Williams**

A DISTINGUISHED THUG STOLE MY HEART I II & III

LOVE SHOULDN'T HURT I II III IV

RENEGADE BOYS I II III IV

PAID IN KARMA I II III

SAVAGE STORMS

By **Meesha**

A GANGSTER'S CODE I &, II III

A GANGSTER'S SYN I II III

THE SAVAGE LIFE I II III

CHAINED TO THE STREETS I II III

By J-Blunt

PUSH IT TO THE LIMIT

By **Bre' Hayes**

BLOOD OF A BOSS **I, II, III, IV, V**

SHADOWS OF THE GAME

By **Askari**

THE STREETS BLEED MURDER **I, II & III**

THE HEART OF A GANGSTA I II& III

By **Jerry Jackson**

CUM FOR ME I II III IV V

An **LDP Erotica Collaboration**

BRIDE OF A HUSTLA **I II & II**

THE FETTI GIRLS **I, II& III**

CORRUPTED BY A GANGSTA I, II III, IV

BLINDED BY HIS LOVE

THE PRICE YOU PAY FOR LOVE

DOPE GIRL MAGIC I II

By **Destiny Skai**

WHEN A GOOD GIRL GOES BAD

By **Adrienne**

THE COST OF LOYALTY I II III

By Kweli

A GANGSTER'S REVENGE **I II III & IV**

THE BOSS MAN'S DAUGHTERS I II III IV V

Meesha

A SAVAGE LOVE **I & II**

BAE BELONGS TO ME I II

A HUSTLER'S DECEIT I, II, III

WHAT BAD BITCHES DO I, II, III

SOUL OF A MONSTER I II III

KILL ZONE

A DOPE BOY'S QUEEN

By **Aryanna**

A KINGPIN'S AMBITON

A KINGPIN'S AMBITION **II**

I MURDER FOR THE DOUGH

By **Ambitious**

TRUE SAVAGE I II III IV V VI

DOPE BOY MAGIC I, II, III

MIDNIGHT CARTEL I II

CITY OF KINGZ

By **Chris Green**

A DOPEBOY'S PRAYER

By **Eddie "Wolf" Lee**

THE KING CARTEL **I, II & III**

By **Frank Gresham**

THESE NIGGAS AIN'T LOYAL **I, II & III**

By **Nikki Tee**

GANGSTA SHYT **I II &III**

By **CATO**

THE ULTIMATE BETRAYAL

By **Phoenix**

BOSS'N UP **I , II & III**

By **Royal Nicole**

I LOVE YOU TO DEATH

Savage Storms

By Destiny J
I RIDE FOR MY HITTA
I STILL RIDE FOR MY HITTA
By **Misty Holt**
LOVE & CHASIN' PAPER
By **Qay Crockett**
TO DIE IN VAIN
SINS OF A HUSTLA
By **ASAD**
BROOKLYN HUSTLAZ
By **Boogsy Morina**
BROOKLYN ON LOCK I & II
By **Sonovia**
GANGSTA CITY
By **Teddy Duke**
A DRUG KING AND HIS DIAMOND I & II III
A DOPEMAN'S RICHES
HER MAN, MINE'S TOO I, II
CASH MONEY HO'S
By Nicole Goosby
TRAPHOUSE KING **I II & III**
KINGPIN KILLAZ I II III
STREET KINGS I II
PAID IN BLOOD **I II**
CARTEL KILLAZ I II III
DOPE GODS
By **Hood Rich**
LIPSTICK KILLAH **I, II, III**
CRIME OF PASSION I II & III
FRIEND OR FOE

Meesha

By **Mimi**
STEADY MOBBN' **I, II, III**
THE STREETS STAINED MY SOUL
By **Marcellus Allen**
WHO SHOT YA **I, II, III**
SON OF A DOPE FIEND
Renta
GORILLAZ IN THE BAY **I II III IV**
TEARS OF A GANGSTA I II
DE'KARI
TRIGGADALE I II III
Elijah R. Freeman
GOD BLESS THE TRAPPERS I, II, III
THESE SCANDALOUS STREETS I, II, III
FEAR MY GANGSTA I, II, III IV
THESE STREETS DON'T LOVE NOBODY I, II
BURY ME A G I, II, III, IV, V
A GANGSTA'S EMPIRE I, II, III, IV
THE DOPEMAN'S BODYGAURD I II
THE REALEST KILLAZ
Tranay Adams
THE STREETS ARE CALLING
Duquie Wilson
MARRIED TO A BOSS... I II III
By Destiny Skai & Chris Green
KINGZ OF THE GAME I II III IV
Playa Ray
SLAUGHTER GANG I II III
RUTHLESS HEART I II III
By Willie Slaughter

192

FUK SHYT

By Blakk Diamond

DON'T F#CK WITH MY HEART I II

By Linnea

ADDICTED TO THE DRAMA I II III

By Jamila

YAYO I II III

A SHOOTER'S AMBITION I II

By S. Allen

TRAP GOD

By Troublesome

FOREVER GANGSTA

GLOCKS ON SATIN SHEETS I II

By Adrian Dulan

TOE TAGZ I II III

By Ah'Million

KINGPIN DREAMS I II

By Paper Boi Rari

CONFESSIONS OF A GANGSTA

By Nicholas Lock

I'M NOTHING WITHOUT HIS LOVE

By Monet Dragun

CAUGHT UP IN THE LIFE I II

By Robert Baptiste

NEW TO THE GAME I II III

By **Malik D. Rice**

LIFE OF A SAVAGE I II III

A GANGSTA'S QUR'AN

By **Romell Tukes**

LOYALTY AIN'T PROMISED

By Keith Williams

QUIET MONEY I II

THUG LIFE

By **Trai'Quan**

THE STREETS MADE ME I II

By **Larry D. Wright**

THE ULTIMATE SACRIFICE I, II, III, IV, V

KHADIFI

IF YOU CROSS ME ONCE

ANGEL I II

By **Anthony Fields**

THE LIFE OF A HOOD STAR

By **Ca$h & Rashia Wilson**

BOOKS BY LDP'S CEO, CA$H

TRUST IN NO MAN

TRUST IN NO MAN 2

TRUST IN NO MAN 3

BONDED BY BLOOD

SHORTY GOT A THUG

THUGS CRY

THUGS CRY 2

THUGS CRY 3

TRUST NO BITCH

TRUST NO BITCH 2

TRUST NO BITCH 3

TIL MY CASKET DROPS

RESTRAINING ORDER

RESTRAINING ORDER 2

IN LOVE WITH A CONVICT

LIFE OF A HOOD STAR

Coming Soon

BONDED BY BLOOD 2

BOW DOWN TO MY GANGSTA

Meesha

CPSIA information can be obtained
at www.ICGtesting.com
Printed in the USA
LVHW051720101120
671307LV00011B/1419